Walter Tevis was born in San Francisco and grew up in Kentucky. He was a professor of English in Ohio, and is now a novelist living in New York City. He is the author of *Mockingbird* (available from Corgi Books) and also of *The Hustler* and *The Man Who Fell To Earth*, both of which became modern classics and were made into films that have gathered a cult following.

'For a . . . satisfactory appreciation of the paradox of time travel, try . . . *The Other End of the Line* which demonstrates that here is an author who can make it work for him. It is one of 13 in *Far From Home* . . . each a little gem by a master of his craft'
The Birmingham Post

'A splendid collection of stories'
Bolton Evening News

Also by Walter Tevis

MOCKINGBIRD

and published by Corgi Books

Far from Home

Walter Tevis

CORGI BOOKS

FAR FROM HOME

A CORGI BOOK 0 552 12404 4

Originally published in Great Britain by Victor Gollancz Ltd.

PRINTING HISTORY

Victor Gollancz edition published 1983
Corgi edition published 1984

Acknowledgements
'Rent Control' copyright © 1979 by Omni Publications International
Ltd.
'The Apotheosis of Myra' copyright © 1980 by Playboy Publications,
Inc.
'Out of Luck' copyright © 1980 by Omni Publications International
Ltd.
'Echo' copyright © 1980 by Mercury Press, Inc.
'The Other End of the Line' copyright © 1961 by Mercury Press, Inc.
'The Big Bounce' copyright © 1958 by Galaxy Publishing Corporation.
'The Goldbrick' originally published as 'Operation Goldbrick'
copyright © 1957 by Quinn Publishing Co.
'The Ifth of Oofth' copyright © 1957 by Galaxy Publishing
Corporation.
'The Scholar's Disciple' copyright © 1969 by the National Council of
Teachers of English.
'Far From Home' copyright © 1958 by Mercury Press, Inc.

This book is set in 10/11 Times

Corgi Books are published by Transworld Publishers Ltd.,
Century House. 61-63 Uxbridge Road. Ealing. London W5 5SA

Printed and bound in Great Britain by
Hunt Barnard Printing Ltd, Aylesbury, Bucks.

For Eleanora, Mimi, Stan, Rosemary,
Bette, Frank, Amy, Lynn, Merle and Herry

Contents

PART ONE

Far From Home

The Other End of the Line

Hungover from cheap whiskey, George Bledsoe made a simple error that many people make: he mistakenly dialed his own number on the telephone. He was attempting to call a girl he knew – a homely girl, but one with the virtues of being quick and easy – and, through his customary impatience and general fogginess, let the wrong pattern of digits govern his pudgy index finger: BE-8-5883.

He did not get the busy signal. He should have; but he did not. Instead, the phone began clicking and an operator's voice announced dimly, as if from a great distance, 'That's a ship-to-shore connection, sir.' George Bledsoe, just then realizing that he *had*, in fact, dialed his own number, said, 'What the hell?' There was a great deal of static and then a man's voice said, 'All right. Who is it?'

George blinked. The voice was loud and arrogant. It sounded somehow familiar, but he could not place it.

But George was not by nature a deferential person. 'Who in hell are *you*, friend?' he said.

The voice paused a moment and then it said, 'This is George Bledsoe.'

'Look, friend,' George Bledsoe said, 'You can take that and . . .' He started to hang up and then stopped. *How could . . .*

'That's right,' the voice said. 'How could I *know*?' And then, 'You let it sink in a minute, George, and then you get that tablet of paper out of the top dresser drawer and get yourself a pencil out of the box on the refrigerator and you get ready to write some things down. We don't have all day.'

George was staring at the phone in disbelief. It *was* his voice, as if on a tape recorder. He blinked, and found himself sweating. But, unused to taking orders, he said, 'Why should I?'

'*Don't argue, dammit.* I'm talking to you from October

ninth. I'm sitting in a boat, twenty-eight miles and two months from where you are and I've got a pile of newspapers, Georgie, that haven't even been printed yet, back there in August where you're talking from. I'm going to make you rich.'

It sounded like a con game. George's eyes narrowed. 'Why should you?'

'Because I'm you, you stupid bastard. Get that paper and start writing. I'm going to give you the names of some racehorses and of three issues of stocks. And a baseball team. You'd better get them right the first time. There won't be another.'

George was staring around the room dizzily; the hand that held the phone was sticky with sweat. 'How can . . . ?'

'Dammit, shut up. *I* don't know how. It just is.'

He got the notepad, and got them all down. Twenty-six racehorses and three stocks and the ball team that was going to win the World Series. Then the phone clicked and the line went dead. Thoroughly dead; he could not even get the dial tone.

There were three horses on his list for the next day. They were all medium-long shots, and they all won. He had started with fifty dollars; he left the track in a kind of cold, glassy-eyed frenzy, with over seven thousand dollars in cash in his pockets. In his shirt pocket, over his heart, was the sheet of notepaper, his greatest gift in the world – a gift from himself.

During the next two months the horses all won at their different tracks and the stocks all split, shot up, declared unexpected dividends. By nosing out the wealthiest bookies at home, in Miami, and in four other cities, and by careful spreading of his bets, George was able to make himself a millionaire after the first five weeks. He won a quarter million on the World Series alone. It was on this last that a bookie who hadn't hedged his bets adequately against George's hundred-thousand-dollar lay-out was forced to offer him his own luxury fishing boat, anchored off Key West, as part payment. George, seeing the

12

handwriting on the wall plainly enough, accepted with what was for him considerable graciousness. That is, he merely called the bookie a chiseling bastard, trimmed five thousand off the boat's evaluation, and took it.

He knew that it was somehow in the nature of things that he must be aboard a boat with a telephone on October ninth. He would be getting a phone call.

The ordaining of it all took no effort on his part. He was called a week later by the telephone company, who wished to know if he planned to continue the ship-to-shore service on the boat. He told them yes, and then, as if it were an after thought, mentioned that he would like his old Miami number transferred to the boat – important friends would be calling. The number? BE-8-5883. Then, when he had bet the final horse on his list, betting the track odds down to the point of diminishing returns, phoning and nagging the nine remaining New York and Chicago bookies who would still take his bets, he hired a chauffeured limousine to take him to Key West. He did not go alone; with him were two attractive young ladies, a gambling friend, a large box of frozen prime steaks, and two cases of twenty-dollar-a-bottle whiskey. And a pile of newspapers.

It was during the ebullient stage of his drunkenness on this automobile ride, after he had tired of needling his friends, that a striking thought occurred to him: what if he decided not to go to the boat at all? His mind fogged at the thought. But how could he *not* be on that boat October ninth? He had, in a sense, already been there. That part of his future was a part of his past, and you couldn't change the past. But you could change the future, couldn't you? He could not understand it. He drank more whiskey and tried to forget about it; it wasn't important anyway. What was important was his twelve-hundred-dollar platinum wristwatch, his two-hundred-dollar shoes, his cashmere jacket, his bank accounts. He had come a long way in those two months. One of the girls, whose name was supposed to be Lili, snuggled up to him. He began playing with her and tried to forget about time paradoxes.

13

The boat looked to George like something out of a Man of Distinction ad; it was big, sleek, polished, and beautifully equipped. His heart swelled with something resembling pride when he surveyed its lines, standing drunkenly on the dock, with a disheveled Lili hanging on his arm. They went aboard, and Lili giggled, and whistled at the mahogany bar, the innerspring mattresses, the hi-fi, the impeccable little stainless steel galley. George, suddenly pensive, left Lili fixing drinks at the bar for the party and went into the boat's little air-conditioned cabin, to look around.

Somehow the sight of it shook him: sitting on a small table, next to a tan leather armchair, was a bright, glossy red telephone. He walked over to it slowly and read the number on the dial. The man from the company had been there, for it read MIAMI: BE-8-5883. Outside on the deck the girls were laughing now, and there was the sound of ice clinking in glasses. Someone called out drunkenly, 'Come on out, Georgie, and have a *bon voyage*.' He didn't answer, still looking at the phone.

A pilot had been hired and he took them out that afternoon. They fished in a desultory way, too drunk and noisy to care. George drank continuously, bullied everyone loudly, made no attempt to fish. A restlessness, an impatience, was eating at him; in his mind telephones were ringing faintly all day. By sundown of the first day they were spent with liquor, sex, sunshine and quarreling. George passed out across the deck, near the one fish that Lili had, miraculously, caught; a small, wide-eyed bonito with a white, flabby belly. The last fleeting thought to enter his mind before he fell into smirking unconsciousness was *Why can't that lousy son of a bitch call me early? Why should I wait? . . .*

The ninth of October was overcast – cold and muggy – as was George's disposition. No one was any longer interested in fishing. The gambler slept; the girls kept to themselves on deck; and George shut himself up in the cabin, waiting for the phone to ring. He swore under his breath occasionally, but otherwise passed the morning in silence. He contemplated the luxury of his silk dressing gown, the brass and mahogany furnishings around him, the good, solid teakwood deck beneath his feet; and the thought of the virtually penniless and belligerent drunkard who was about to call him from a crumby little beach house in Miami. At his feet sat the pile of newspapers, opened to the sporting pages. He looked down at them now and swore. He was beginning to sweat.

Outside the cabin window the sky was dead white, hanging thickly over the cold green Atlantic horizon. They were ninety miles out from shore, the pilot had said. George continued drinking, angry now at himself – the other himself – for not having bothered to mention the time of day his call had been received. He had dialed the number at about two in the afternoon; but of course that didn't mean that two o'clock was the time it was received, two months later. He continued looking at his watch and at the telephone and at his watch again, drinking. Occasionally he would look out the window at the serenely violent ocean, ice green beneath the fishbelly sky, and curse.

And then, just before two o'clock, an idea struck him, a very simple idea: Why should *he* wait? He would make the call himself. He had never, in the two months since it had happened, tried dialing his own number again – why had he never thought of it? Why should he wait for that poor slob of a hungover George Bledsoe to call *him* – him with his private fishing boat and his twenty-dollar whiskey?

He picked up the phone angrily, with thick fingers, and began dialing: BE-8-5883. He was breathing heavily. After the last digit the phone began to buzz, ringing. He smiled sweatily and leaned back in his chair. Then there was a *click* and a voice answered. 'Hello?'

He sat bolt upright in his chair. It was a woman's voice.

He hesitated and then said, 'Hello.' *Could he have dialed the wrong number?* 'What number is this?'

The voice was that of an old woman, quavery but matter-of-fact. 'This is BE-8-5883. Mrs Arthur Cavanaugh talking.'

'Oh.' He took a quick sip from his drink. 'Is . . . is George Bledsoe there?'

'No. No, he isn't.' There seemed to be some hesitation in her voice. 'Mr Bledsoe hasn't lived in this house for some time.'

Abruptly he felt relieved – he had probably only moved to a bigger home. About time, anyway, but why had he been frightened of this old bat on the phone?

The woman was saying querulously, 'Are you a friend . . . of Mr Bledsoe's?'

He laughed suddenly, coarsely. 'That's right, lady. I'm a friend of Mr Bledsoe's.'

'Well, I don't know just how to tell you this,' the woman said, 'but a person would have thought you'd read about it in the papers. It was in all the papers. They found Mr Bledsoe's body, stark naked, a hundred miles out in the Gulf. It was about two months ago they found him, and the thing is there's nobody yet knows how he got out there.'

He sat silent for what seemed a very long time. There was a faint clicking in the phone, but he ignored this. The woman must be mistaken. An old fool. A bitch. Although the cabin was tightly closed, he felt the distinct sensation of a cold wind blowing on the back of his neck. Shaking himself, he gathered his voice together. The woman was a lying bitch. 'How George Bledsoe got out there, lady, was in his private boat,' he said, more to himself than to her. 'The same way he's gonna get back to shore. In his private boat.'

The wind on the back of his neck was stronger now, and he was shivering. The wind seemed to be penetrating his clothes, even, blowing through his dressing gown, through the tailored silk shirt beneath it. Dimly, as if from a great and dreadful distance, he heard the old woman's voice saying, 'Why, Mr Bledsoe never had a boat, Lord forbid. Mr Bledsoe was a poor man . . .'

Abruptly he leaned forward, shouting. '*No.* No, you rotten bitch!' and he slammed the phone back in its cradle. It was cold in the room. He was shivering. There

16

was a bright, grayish light in the cabin, getting brighter. He grabbed the phone again, shaking, and dialed *O*, for the operator. The dial felt soft to his finger, squashy.

The operator's voice came, faint. 'Ship-to-shore service.'

His voice was hoarse, strange in his ears. 'This is Bledsoe. BE-8-5883. Is there a call for me?'

'No, sir. Or, yes, there was a call.'

'From who?' It took an effort to keep from shouting – or screaming.

'Just a moment.' And then, 'That's odd, sir; it must be an error. I have the number calling listed as BE-8-5883. And that's your number, sir.'

'My God, I know. Put the call through.'

Her voice was fainter, fading away from him. 'I'm sorry, you'll have to wait until the party calls again. When he called, a few moments ago, the line was busy . . .' The last words were so faint that he could hardly hear them. He was screaming when she finished, *'Put the call through, God damn it, put the call through.'*

From the receiver her voice was the minute thread of a whisper, but he heard it plainly. 'I'm sorry sir, the line was busy.'

And then the phone went altogether dead.

Then, after sitting for a moment with his eyes shut against the impossible white daylight in the closed cabin, his body huddled against the cold wind that was blowing through the bulkheads of the rich man's boat that he could not possibly have been in, blowing coldly against his body through the rich man's clothes that he, George Bledsoe, could not possibly have afforded, he took a deep breath and opened his eyes, looking down.

Below him, through the fading, now translucent teakwood deck, he could see the flat, ice-green water of the Atlantic Ocean, ninety miles from shore.

The Big Bounce

'Let me show you something,' Farnsworth said. He set his near-empty drink – a Bacardi martini – on the mantel and waddled out of the room toward the basement.

I sat in my big leather chair, feeling very peaceful with the world, watching the fire. Whatever Farnsworth would have to show tonight would be far more entertaining than watching TV – my custom on other evenings. Farnsworth, with his four labs in the house and his very tricky mind, never failed to provide my best night of the week.

When he returned, after a moment, he had with him a small box, about three inches square. He held this carefully in one hand and stood by the fireplace dramatically – or as dramatically as a very small, very fat man with pink cheeks can stand by a fireplace of the sort that seems to demand a big man with tweeds, pipe and, perhaps, a saber wound.

Anyway, he held the box dramatically and he said, 'Last week, I was playing around in the chem lab, trying to make a new kind of rubber eraser. Did quite well with the other drafting equipment, you know, especially the dimensional curve and the photosensitive ink. Well, I approached the job by trying for a material that would absorb graphite without abrading paper.'

I was a little disappointed with this; it sounded pretty tame. But I said, 'How did it come out?'

He screwed his pudgy face up thoughtfully. 'Synthesized the material, all right, and it seems to work, but the interesting thing is that it has a certain – ah – secondary property that would make it quite awkward to use. Interesting property, though. Unique, I am inclined to believe.'

This began to sound more like it. 'And what property is

that?' I poured myself a shot of straight rum from the bottle sitting on the table beside me. I did not like straight rum, but I preferred it to Farnsworth's imaginative cocktails.

'I'll show you, John,' he said. He opened the box and I could see that it was packed with some kind of batting. He fished in this and withdrew a gray ball about the size of a golf ball and set the box on the mantel.

'And that's the – eraser?' I asked.

'Yes,' he said. Then he squatted down, held the ball about a half-inch from the floor, and dropped it.

It bounced, naturally enough. Then it bounced again. And again. Only this was not natural, for on the second bounce the ball went higher in the air than on the first, and on the third bounce higher still. After a half minute, my eyes were bugging out and the little ball was bouncing four feet in the air and going higher each time.

I grabbed my glass. 'What the hell!' I said.

Farnsworth caught the ball in a pudgy hand and held it. He was smiling a little sheepishly. 'Interesting effect, isn't it?'

'Now wait a minute,' I said, beginning to think about it. 'What's the gimmick? What kind of motor do you have in that thing?'

His eyes were wide and a little hurt. 'No gimmick, John. None at all. Just a very peculiar molecular structure.'

'Structure!' I said. 'Bouncing balls just don't pick up energy out of nowhere. I don't care how their molecules are put together. And you don't get energy out without putting energy in.'

'Oh,' he said, 'that's the really interesting thing. Of course you're right; energy *does* go into the ball. Here, I'll show you.'

He let the ball drop again and it began bouncing, higher and higher, until it was hitting the ceiling. Farnsworth reached out to catch it, but he fumbled and the thing danced off his hand, hit the mantelpiece and zipped across the room. It banged into the far wall, ricocheted, ranked off three other walls, picking up speed all the time.

19

When it whizzed by me like a rifle bullet, I began to get worried, but it hit against one of the heavy draperies by the window and this damped its motion enough so that it fell to the floor.

It started bouncing again immediately, but Farnsworth scrambled across the room and grabbed it. He was perspiring a little and he began instantly to transfer the ball from one hand to another and back again as if it were hot.

'Here,' he said, and handed it to me.

I almost dropped it.

'It's like a ball of ice!' I said. 'Have you been keeping it in the refrigerator?'

'No. As a matter of fact, it was at room temperature a few minutes ago.'

'Now wait a minute,' I said. 'I only teach physics in high school, but I know better than that. Moving around in warm air doesn't make anything cold except by evaporation.'

'Well, there's your input and output, John,' he said. 'The ball lost heat and took on motion. Simple conversion.'

My jaw must have dropped to my waist. 'Do you mean that that little thing is converting heat to kinetic energy?'

'Apparently.'

'But that's impossible!'

He was beginning to smile thoughtfully. The ball was not as cold now as it had been and I was holding it in my lap.

'A steam engine does it,' he said, 'and a steam turbine. Of course, they're not very efficient.'

'They work mechanically, too, and only because water expands when it turns to steam.'

'This seems to do it differently,' he said, sipping thoughtfully at his dark-brown martini. 'I don't know exactly how – maybe something piezo-electric about the way its molecules slide about. I ran some tests – measured its impact energy in foot pounds and compared that with the heat loss in BTUs. Seemed to be about 98 percent efficient, as close as I could tell. Apparently it converts heat into bounce very well. Interesting, isn't it?'

'*Interesting*?' I almost came flying out of my chair. My mind was beginning to spin like crazy. 'If you're not pulling my leg with this thing, Farnsworth, you've got something by the tail there that's just a little bit bigger than the discovery of fire.'

He blushed modestly. 'I'd rather thought that myself,' he admitted.

'Good Lord, look at the heat that's available!' I said, getting really excited now.

Farnsworth was still smiling, very pleased with himself. 'I suppose you could put this thing in a box, with convection fins, and let it bounce around inside—'

'I'm way ahead of you,' I said. 'But that wouldn't work. All your kinetic energy would go right back to heat, on impact – and eventually that little ball would build up enough speed to blast its way through any box you could build.'

'Then how would you work it?'

'Well,' I said, choking down the rest of my rum, 'you'd seal the ball in a big steel cylinder, attach the cylinder to a crankshaft and flywheel, give the thing a shake to start the ball bouncing back and forth, and let it run like a gasoline engine or something. It would get all the heat it needed from the air in a normal room. Mount the apparatus in your house and it would pump your water, operate a generator and keep you cool at the same time!'

I sat down again, shakily, and began pouring myself another drink.

Farnsworth had taken the ball from me and was carefully putting it back in its padded box. He was visibly showing excitement, too; I could see that his cheeks were ruddier and his eyes even brighter than normal. 'But what if you want the cooling and don't have any work to be done?'

'Simple,' I said. 'You just let the machine turn a

flywheel or lift weights and drop them, or something like that, outside your house. You have an air intake inside. And if, in the winter, you don't want to lose heat, you just mount the thing in an outside building, attach it to your generator and use the power to do whatever you want – heat your house, say. There's plenty of heat in the outside air even in December.'

'John,' said Farnsworth, 'you are very ingenious. It might work.'

'Of course it'll work.' Pictures were beginning to light up in my head. 'And don't you realize that this is the answer to the solar power problem? Why, mirrors and selenium are, at best, ten percent efficient! Think of big pumping stations on the Sahara! All that heat, all that need for power, for irrigation!' I paused a moment for effect. 'Farnsworth, this can change the very shape of the earth!'

Farnsworth seemed to be lost in thought. Finally he looked at me strangely and said, 'Perhaps we had better try to build a model.'

I was so excited by the thing that I couldn't sleep that night. I kept dreaming of power stations, ocean liners, even automobiles, being operated by balls bouncing back and forth in cylinders.

I even worked out a spaceship in my mind, a bullet-shaped affair with a huge rubber ball on its end, gyroscopes to keep it oriented properly, the ball serving as solution to that biggest of missile-engineering problems, excess heat. You'd build a huge concrete launching field, supported all the way down to bedrock, hop in the ship and start bouncing. Of course it would be kind of a rough ride . . .

In the morning, I called my superintendent and told him to get a substitute for the rest of the week; I was going to be busy.

Then I started working in the machine shop in Farnsworth's basement, trying to turn out a working model of a device that, by means of a crankshaft, oleo dampers and a reciprocating cylinder, would pick up some of that random kinetic energy from the bouncing ball and do something useful with it, like turning a drive shaft. I was just working out a convection-and-air-pump system for circulating hot air around the ball when Farnsworth came in.

He had a sphere of about the size of a basketball and, if he had made it to my specifications, weighing thirty-five pounds. He had a worried frown on his forehead.

'It looks good,' I said. 'What's the trouble?'

'There seems to be a slight hitch,' he said. 'I've been testing for conductivity. It seems to be quite low.'

'That's what I'm working on now. It's just a mechanical problem of pumping enough warm air back to the ball. We can do it with no more than a twenty percent efficiency loss. In an engine, that's nothing.'

'Maybe you're right. But this material conducts heat even less than rubber does.'

'The little ball yesterday didn't seem to have any trouble.' I said.

'Naturally not. It had had plenty of time to warm up before I started it. And its mass-surface area relationship was pretty low – the larger you make a sphere, of course, the more mass inside in proportion to the outside area.'

'You're right, but I think we can whip it. We may have to honeycomb the ball and have the machine operate a hot-air pump; but we can work it out.'

All that day, I worked with lathe, milling machine and hacksaw. After clamping the new big ball securely to a workbench, Farnsworth pitched in to help me. But we weren't able to finish by nightfall and Farnsworth turned his spare bedroom over to me for the night. I was too tired to go home.

And too tired to sleep soundly, too. Farnsworth lived on the edge of San Francisco, by a big truck bypass, and almost all night I wrestled with the pillow and sheets, listening half-consciously to those heavy trucks rumbling by, and in my mind, always that little gray ball, bouncing and bouncing and bouncing . . .

At daybreak, I abruptly came fully awake with the sound of crashing echoing in my ears, a battering sound that seemed to come from the basement. I grabbed my shirt and pants, rushed out of the room, almost knocked over Farnsworth, who was struggling to get his shoes on out in the hall, and we scrambled down the two flights of stairs together.

The place was a chaos, battered and bashed equipment everywhere, and on the floor, overturned against the far wall, the table that the ball had been clamped to. The ball itself was gone.

I had not been fully asleep all night, and the sight of that mess, and what it meant, jolted me immediately awake. Something, probably a heavy truck, had started a tiny oscillation in that ball. And the ball had been heavy enough to start the table bouncing with it until, by dancing that table around the room, it had literally torn the clamp off and shaken itself free. What had happened afterward was obvious, with the ball building up velocity with every successive bounce.

But where was the ball now?

Suddenly Farnsworth cried out hoarsely, 'Look!' and I followed his outstretched, pudgy finger to where, at one side of the basement, a window had been broken open – a small window, but plenty big enough for something the size of a basketball to crash through it.

There was a little weak light coming from outdoors. And then I saw the ball. It was in Farnsworth's backyard, bouncing a little sluggishly on the grass. The grass would damp it, hold it back, until we could get to it. Unless . . .

I took off up the basement steps like a streak. Just beyond the backyard, I had caught a glimpse of something that frightened me. A few yards from where I had seen the ball was the edge of the big six-lane highway, a broad ribbon of smooth, hard concrete.

I got through the house to the back porch, rushed out and was in the backyard just in time to see the ball take its first bounce onto the concrete. I watched it, fascinated,

24

when it hit – after the soft, energy-absorbing turf, the concrete was like a springboard. Immediately the ball flew high in the air. I was running across the yard toward it, praying under my breath, *Fall on that grass next time*.

It hit before I got to it, and right on the concrete again, and this time I saw it go straight up at least fifty feet.

My mind was suddenly full of thoughts of dragging mattresses from the house, or making a net or something to stop that hurtling thirty-five pounds; but I stood where I was, unable to move, and saw it come down again on the highway. It went up a hundred feet. And down again on the concrete, about fifteen feet further down the road. In the direction of the city.

That time it was two hundred feet, and when it hit again, it made a thud that you could have heard for a quarter of a mile. I could practically see it flatten out on the road before it took off upward again, at twice the speed it had hit at.

Suddenly generating an idea, I whirled and ran back to Farnsworth's house. He was standing in the yard now, shivering from the morning air, looking at me like a little lost and badly scared child.

'Where are your car keys?' I shouted at him.

'In my pocket.'

'Come on!'

I took him by the arm and half dragged him to the carport. I got the keys from him, started the car, and by mangling about seven traffic laws and three rosebushes, managed to get on the highway, facing in the direction that the ball was heading.

'Look,' I said, trying to drive down the road and search for the ball at the same time. 'It's risky, but if I can get the car under it and we can hop out in time, it should crash through the roof. That ought to slow it down enough for us to nab it.'

'But – what about my car?' Farnsworth bleated.

'What about that first building – or first person – it hits in San Francisco?'

'Oh,' he said. 'Hadn't thought of that.'

I slowed the car and stuck my head out the window. It was lighter now, but no sign of the ball. 'If it happens to get to town – any town, for that matter – it'll be falling from about ten or twenty miles. Or forty.'

'Maybe it'll go high enough first so that it'll burn. Like a meteor.'

'No chance,' I said. 'Built-in cooling system, remember?'

Farnsworth formed his mouth into an 'Oh' and exactly at that moment there was a resounding *thump* and I saw the ball hit in a field, maybe twenty yards from the edge of the road, and take off again. This time it didn't seem to double its velocity, and I figured the ground was soft enough to hold it back – but it wasn't slowing down either, not with a bounce factor of better than two to one.

Without watching for it to go up, I drove as quickly as I could off the road and over – carrying part of a wire fence with me – to where it had hit. There was no mistaking it; there was a depression about three feet deep, like a small crater.

I jumped out of the car and stared up. It took me a few seconds to spot it, over my head. One side caught by the pale and slanting morning sunlight, it was only a bright diminishing speck.

The car motor was running and I waited until the ball disappeared for a moment and then reappeared. I watched for another couple of seconds until I felt I could make a decent guess on its direction, shouted at Farnsworth to get out of the car – it had just occurred to me that there was no use risking his life, too – dove in and drove a hundred yards or so to the spot I had anticipated.

I stuck my head out the window and up. The ball was the size of an egg now. I adjusted the car's position, jumped out and ran for my life.

It hit instantly after – about sixty feet from the car. And at the same time, it occurred to me that what I was trying to do was completely impossible. Better to hope that the ball hit a pond, or bounced out to sea, or landed in a sand

26

dune. All we could do would be to follow, and if it ever was damped down enough, grab it.

It had hit soft ground and didn't double its height that time, but it had still gone higher. It was out of sight for almost a lifelong minute.

And then – incredibly rotten luck – it came down, with an ear-shattering thwack, on the concrete highway again. I had seen it hit, and instantly afterward I saw a crack as wide as a finger open along the entire width of the road. And the ball had flown back up like a rocket.

My God, I was thinking, *now it means business. And on the next bounce . . .*

It seemed like an incredibly long time that we craned our necks, Farnsworth and I, watching for it to reappear in the sky. And when it finally did, we could hardly follow it. It whistled like a bomb and we saw the gray streak come plummeting to earth almost a quarter of a mile away from where we were standing.

But we didn't see it go back up again.

For a moment, we stared at each other silently. Then Farnsworth almost whispered, 'Perhaps it's landed in a pond.'

'Or in the world's biggest cowpile,' I said. 'Come on!'

We could have met our deaths by rock salt and buckshot that night, if the farmer who owned that field had been home. We tore up everything we came to getting across it – including cabbages and rhubarb. But we had to search for ten minutes, and even then we didn't find the ball.

What we found was a hole in the ground that could have been a small-scale meteor crater. It was a good twenty feet deep. But at the bottom, no ball.

I stared wildly at it for a full minute before I focused my eyes enough to see, at the bottom, a thousand little gray fragments.

And immediately it came to both of us at the same time. A poor conductor, the ball had used up all its available heat on that final impact. Like a golf ball that has been dipped in liquid air and dropped, it had smashed into thin splinters.

The hole had sloping sides and I scrambled down in it and picked up one of the pieces, using my handkerchief, folded – there was no telling just how cold it would be.

It was the stuff, all right. And colder than an icicle. I climbed out. 'Let's go home,' I said.

Farnsworth looked at me thoughtfully. Then he sort of cocked his head to one side and asked, 'What do you suppose will happen when those pieces thaw?'

I stared at him. I began to think of a thousand tiny slivers whizzing around erratically, richocheting off buildings, in downtown San Francisco and in twenty counties, and no matter what they hit, moving and accelerating as long as there was any heat in the air to give them energy.

And then I saw a tool shed, on the other side of the pasture from us.

But Farnsworth was ahead of me, waddling along puffing. He got the shovels out and handed one to me.

We didn't say a word, neither of us, for hours. It takes a long time to fill a hole twenty feet deep – especially when you're shoveling very, very carefully and packing down the dirt very, very hard.

The Goldbrick

Two army engineers found it while drilling a hole through one of the Appalachian Mountains, in the Primitive Reservation, on a lovely spring day in 1993. The hole was to be used for a monorail track; and although in 1993 it was very simple to run monorail lines *over* mountains, it was also quite easy to drill large, straight holes through almost anything; and the US Army liked to effect the neatness of straight lines. So the engineers had set up a little converter machine on a tripod, pointed it, and proceeded to convert a singularly neat hole, twenty-two feet in diameter, in the side of the mountain. At first the mountain converted nicely, the hole tunneling along at an efficient thirteen feet per hour; and the engineers, whose names were George and Sam, were quite pleased with themselves and rubbed their hands together with pleasure; while the little machine on the tripod hummed merrily, birds sang, and wisps of brown smoke floated off from the mountain into an otherwise clear blue sky.

And then they found it. Or, rather, the converter did, by abruptly ceasing to convert. The machine continued to hum; but the little feedback-controlled counter, which normally clicked off the number of tons of material substance that had been converted into immaterial substance, stopped. The last wisps of smoke disappeared from the mountainside. The two engineers looked at one another. After a minute George picked a rock up from the ground, a large one, and threw it out in front of the lens of the machine. The rock vanished instantly. The one-tenth ton counter wheel trembled, and was still.

'Well,' Sam said, after a minute. 'It's still working.'

George thought about this for a minute. Then he said, 'I guess we'd better look at the tunnel.'

So they shut the machine off, walked over to the hole in

the mountainside and went in. Fortunately the sun was behind them and they had no difficulty seeing as they made their way down the glassy-smooth shaft – which needed no shoring since the converter had been set to convert part of the materials removed into a quite sturdy lining of neo-adamant. The shaft ended in a forbidding, twenty-two foot, black disk of unconverted mountain bowels. The two of them peered uneasily at this for a few minutes and then Sam said, 'What's this?' and kneeled down to inspect a rectangle, gold in color, about ten inches long and four high, which appeared to be engraved in the rock at the dead end of the tunnel.

'Let me see.' George said, stooping beside his co-scientist and pulling from his pocket a pocketknife, with which he proceeded to scrape around the edges of the rectangle. Some of the loose rock crumbled away, revealing that the rectangle was, actually, one surface of a solid bar of some sort.

He continued to scrape for a few minutes, removing enough rock to get a grip on the sides of the bar with his fingers, took a good hold and began to try to work the bar loose. The other engineer helped him, and they pulled, strained, wedged and pushed for about ten minutes, until finally George said, 'It won't move,' and they stopped, perspiring. And it hadn't moved, not a millimeter.

The two of them glared, for a moment, at the smooth surface of the golden bar, which shone, lustrous, back at them. Then Sam said, 'Let's get a pick.'

'A pick?'

Sam, who knew something of Army history, was patronizing. 'Yes. A kind of manual-powered converter.'

George was impressed. 'But where?' he said.

'At U-10 Supply.'

They left the uncompleted tunnel, stepped into their Minnijet, field model, officer-type helicopter and flew at a leisurely five hundred miles per hour to U-10. U-10 had been, before the 1980s Decade of Enlightenment, the University of Tennessee – the 1980s had held no illusions about what was important to the American Way of Life –

and they landed their little olive-drab plastic craft in front
of the library. Inside, the librarian, a young sergeant, was
put into something of a tizzy at their request for a pick,
and explained to them that the library shelves held only
weapons of the past, and, as far as he knew, there was no
such weapon as a *pick*. He sent them to the captain.

The captain knew what a pick was, all right; but when
the two engineers told him what it was for he called the
major. The major was a tall, athletic officer with wavy
hair, a very neat mustache, a firm, undaunted jaw, and
clear eyes that looked squarely into the future. He smoked
a pipe, of course, and was wearing a natty black field
uniform with regulation crimson cummerbund and beret.
His voice was friendly but there was a 'no-nonsense' tone
in it. 'What's the deal, men?' he said out of the side of his
mouth, the other side being engaged in biting, squarely,
on his pipestem.

They told him about the gold bar.

'Interesting,' he said. 'Let's have a look-see.' And he
sent for a pick, a heavy-duty converter, a portable lighting
system, two quarts of synthetic scotch and three privates.
All of these were stowed away in a staff helicopter and
then the three officers – the two engineers and the major –
flew to the mountains. This being a staff helicopter, the
trip took three and one-half minutes.

At the mountain, two of the privates set up the portable
lighting system in the tunnel while the other studied the
manual that had come with the pick. The major was first
charmed, and then somewhat piqued, by the bar, after
trying to prod it loose with his pipestem. The private with
the pick was called, and after some difficulty with
determining the proper stance and grip for swinging that
instrument – the private was a recent recruit of only
fourteen and naturally knew nothing whatever about
manual converters of any sort – a few desultory swings
were taken at the granite surrounding the bar. After a
while the other two privates joined in, alternating in
swinging the pick, until, finally, a rough area of about two

or three square feet had been hollowed out around the bar, which was found at that time to extend only about four inches back into the mountain. Above the bar they noticed a sort of fissure, like a cicatrice, in the granite; and one of the privates remarked that it looked like the mountain either had been split open to admit the bar from the top, or that, maybe, the bar had just been there and the mountain had grown up around it.

It was impossible to cut away the rock on the other side, so the three privates got a strong grip on the bar and began to pull. Then the officers began to pull on the privates. The bar stayed where it was. They pulled harder. The bar stayed. The major took off his cummerbund and beret and began to sweat. The bar didn't move. The major began to curse, pushed the others aside, grabbed the pick handle, gave a mighty heave, and hit the bar solidly with the point. There was no sound from the impact, and the pick did not rebound, nor did the bar move. The major tried again. And again. Then they knelt and looked at the bar. It still gleamed. No scars.

The major swore for five minutes. Then he said, 'Who owns this mountain?'

George spoke up, 'The Army, sir. Of course.'

'Good,' said the major, beginning to look undaunted again. 'We'll get at that son of a bitch.'

'How, sir?'

'We'll convert this goddamn mountain, that's how.' The major began wrapping his cummerbund back around his waist.

'The whole *mountain*?' Sam said, aghast.

'Level it.' The major dusted off his beret and replaced it.

Sam spoke up querulously, 'But wouldn't that be . . . ah . . . misusing our natural resources, sir?'

'Nonsense. This mountain belongs to the Army. It's not a natural resource. As a matter of fact, it's an eyesore. I order you to vaporize it.'

So they vaporized the mountain. Since the converter could not cut through the bar they set it up – the heavy-duty one – to shear off the top of the mountain. Then they moved the machine around to each of the four sides and sliced them off. Their instruments were very accurate, and when the last wisp of smoke had drifted away there stood in the middle of a plain so smooth billiards could have been played on it, sitting on a neat, rectangular column of granite, four feet high, what was now plainly seen as a shiny, gold colored brick, its sides glittering in the evening sun.

The major picked up the pick and walked slowly over to the column. There was a slight, almost unnoticeable swagger in his walk. He hefted the pick slowly, carefully, braced himself, and took aim. 'All right, you son of a bitch,' he said, and then gave the pick a magnificent swing.

The brick didn't move.

The major stood where he was, looking at the brick, for about three minutes. Then he said, softly, 'All right. *All right*!'

He walked back to the converter – which was sitting on its tripod nearby – and began to adjust its aim and elevation and set its dials, all very carefully. When he was ready he stood behind it, his feet planted firmly, his fists clenched, his lower jaw firm and jutting, his eyes squarely ahead, focused on the brick.

'*Now*!' he said, and pressed the switch. There was a small hum and a tiny puff of smoke and the little column of granite disappeared. The brick was now unsupported and the major watched it, his eyes now betraying an intense gleam, waiting for it to fall to the earth. The major waited.

The brick stayed exactly where it was, four feet above the ground, completely unsupported.

It took the major a few minutes to realize that there was no use in waiting. He said nothing, however; but stepped over to the brick, looked at it a minute, and then reached casually over to it and pushed it, with his index finger. It didn't move. Then the major sat down on the ground and began to cry, very softly, as the sun sank in the west.

That, of course, was only the beginning of it. Within two weeks the little plain that had once been a mountain was covered with multicolored plastic. Quonset huts through which moved so many people of such world-shaking importance that four gossip columnists had to be flown in from New York and Los Angeles to handle the overflow. Generals and admirals abounded, offering careful and profound opinions freely; slim, dark, intense young men with impeccable dark civilian suits and carrying dark attaché cases held hurried, *sotto voce* conferences; reporters did Profiles of everybody. The weather held fair, the neighborhood abounded in divers kinds of nature: birdsong and waterfall, poplar and mountain daisy, which most of the visitors found quaint and novel, and a good time was being had by all.

In the midst of this activity floated the still shiny golden brick, unperturbed, apparently as oblivious of the melee it had attracted as it was of the immutable laws governing the motion of masses: the laws of inertia and reaction, and the law of universal gravitation.

Some interesting things had been discovered about the brick. It was, for instance, completely impervious to any known form of radiant energy; it neither absorbed nor radiated heat; electron microscopes found its surface, on the atomic level, still smooth, metallic and shiny, without gaps; it apparently had no molecular – or, even, atomic – structure to speak of; it would conduct neither electricity, heat, nor anything else; and it obeyed no physical laws whatever. Thus far nine neo-adamant points, sharpened to submicroscopic pointedness and under pressures ranging up to three hundred fifty thousand tons, had failed to make any scratches in its surface; and all had eventually cracked.

The major had recovered most of his old poise and undauntedness, although his eyes now seemed to face the future with some hint of trepidation, and he was assigned to Operation Gold Brick – as the Army had cleverly named it – in an advisory capacity. In fact it was he who gave voice to a notion that had been whispered about for several days. After the ninth neo-adamant point had split against the surface of the brick it was he who marched to the orange Quonset of General Pomeroy and said, 'Sir, let's try an H-bomb.'

So they H-bombed it.

There was some confusion during the four days while the crater was being filled in; but after that was done and new Quonsets were built the Operation was even more pleasant and roomy, since nine more mountains had been leveled by the bomb, and about twenty others had been fused into interesting colors and shapes. The birds and trees and suchlike had, of course, been obliterated; but they had been beginning to pall on the visitors anyway; and now the area had something of the look of a neo-Surrealist landscape, or a Japanese garden. The radiation had, of course, been absorbed by the usual means.

The brick stayed right where it was, its surface parallel to the horizon, poised, immediately after the blast, over a crater two hundred and ninety-four feet deep.

After the failure of the H-bomb the generals' pique and frustration began to turn to anger and, in some cases, fear. One pacifistic lieutenant general did in fact suggest that the brick be left alone and the monorail rerouted; but it was to the credit of the Army that his superiors rallied together and denounced his defeatism for what it was. But the generals did agree at this conference to call in a theoretical physicist, provided one could be found, in a desperate hope that some light might be thrown on the nature of their adversary.

A call was sent out to headquarters at Big-H (once Harvard University) and a two-day scramble ensued while a theory man – or 'egghead' as such men were cleverly called – was sought. One was eventually found, working in a weather observatory in the Kentucky Reservation, and he was brought – a gray-haired old fellow who freely admitted that he read books and refused to drink synthetic whiskey – to the site of the brick, which he surveyed with some attention.

'Well?' said one of the generals.

'Very interesting,' said the theoretical physicist, whose name was Albert, and he produced from a trunk he had brought with him a collection of peculiar-looking instruments, which he began to set up on the ground. After peering down various tripod-mounted tubes, first at the brick and then at the sun, he then said, 'Amazing!'

'Yes,' said one of the generals. 'We know that.' There was a ring of generals in brilliant tunics and of security men in black flannel suits around the physicist.

'Amazing,' he said again. 'This seems to be the exact set point of Propkofski's principle!' He gazed at the brick reverently.

'*Whose* principle?' said one of the security men, raising his eyebrows and fetching a little black book from his breast pocket.

'Propkofski.' The physicist's eyes were aglow. The security men were raising eyebrows at one another. 'The principle of terrestrial orbital space-time suspension, formulated in 1987, I believe. This is the place, gentlemen, the *exact* point, where Propkofski maintained that the mass-influx lines of the Earth's field intersected. This is the very hub, provided that Propkofski was right,' and he pointed to the brick. 'Yet I believe that Propkofski said something about a mountain hindering his observations.'

'Yes?' said the general. 'We removed the mountain.'

'My!' said the old physicist, looking up from the brick for the first time, 'How did you do that? With faith?'

'With a converter,' the general said. 'But what about that brick? How do we move it?'

'The brick? Oh.' The scientist went to the floating piece of golden metal, still unmarred by the H-bomb, and examined it carefully. When he had finished checking it with a good many instruments, mechanical and electronic, he said, 'I wish Newton could see this.'

The security man's eyebrows went up again. 'Newton?'

The old man smiled at him, 'Another physicist,' he said 'Dead.'

'Oh,' said the security man. 'Sorry.'

'So,' said the general, impatiently. 'How do we move it?'

The old man looked at him a moment. 'I suggest you don't.'

'Thank you,' said the general, crisply. 'Then how would you say it *might* be moved?'

The physicist scratched his head. 'Well,' he said, 'I suppose the Earth might be pushed away from it, since it seems to be a kind of Archimedes' fulcrum. A pressure of about seventeen trillion tons per square centimeter might accomplish that. Of course, moving the Earth might alter the length of the year considerably. And then, again, if Propkofski's principle, which states . . .'

'Thank you,' said the general. 'That will be all.'

After the security men had taken the physicist away for investigation the general who had interviewed him looked at another general and then at the others. He could tell they were all having the same wild surmise. Finally, he said, 'Well, why not?'

'Ah . . .' said one of the others.

'The cold war's been going on for fifty years. We may never get a chance to try it out.'

'Ah . . . well . . .'

One of the other, younger generals could not contain himself and abruptly spoke up. 'Let's use it!' he said, his voice quivering with emotion.

And all the rest of them began to chime in, their eagerness, now that one of their number had committed himself, unrepressed. 'Let's use it!' they said. 'Let's use the R-bomb!'

First a pit was dug – or converted – a mile and a half deep and three miles in diameter. This was then filled with neo-adamant except for a hole in the center four by ten inches rectangular, directly under the brick. Then the R-bomb and its electronic detonator, the whole thing about the size and color of an avocado, was lowered into the hole, and then the neo-adamant walls were built up six feet

37

above the ground to enclose the brick in what amounted to the barrel of a monstrous cannon. The states of Virginia, West Virginia, Ohio and half of Kentucky were then evacuated, and a final check was made of the figures. It was determined that the kickback from the blast would throw the Earth approximately four hundred and ten miles out of her orbit, and shorten the length of the year to three hundred and sixty-three days, a number which all of the generals found to be eminently satisfactory, in fact, a decided improvement.

The generals decided to use the old physicist's weather station, in the Kentucky Reservation, as their observation point, its elevation and its distance from the brick being quite desirable.

The station was raised on a tripod to a height of one thousand feet, and the Army had the whole structure properly reinforced and shielded. Then the equipment for observation, the TV monitoring screens and the electron telescopes, was set up and the generals moved in. The old physicist had by this time taken a loyalty oath and he was allowed to remain in the observation dome for the event since, after all, he worked there.

At zero hour minus sixty seconds the senior general carefully pressed a small red button and unwittingly echoed the words of a forgotten subordinate. 'We'll blast the son of a bitch sky high,' he said. Flashbulbs popped. A counter began ticking off the seconds, loudly, efficiently. All eyes were on the large TV screen, which showed the huge circle of white neo-adamant four hundred miles away. The TV picture was being beamed from a satellite eighty miles above the location of the brick; they would be able to see the actual blast before the camera was destroyed. The physicist busied himself with his own instruments, making readings of the sun's position. The seconds ticked off.

At the sixtieth tick the counter became silent. There was no sound in the little observation tower. The white circle on the screen was unchanged. Then, suddenly, the screen erupted. In a burst of flame and steam the neo-adamant circle began to crumble. Flames shot up everywhere. Mountains seen at the edge of the screen began to sizzle and ooze out of shape. It was at this moment that the states of Virginia, West Virginia and Ohio were obliterated. Then, abruptly, the picture changed. A specially controlled monitoring camera had picked up a flash of gold. The brick. It appeared to be flying through the air.

'By God,' said the senior general. 'We did it!'

At this moment the screen went black. There was a roar, a rumble, starting from what seemed to be the very bowels of the Earth, building to a dynamic, deep-buried scream, a screeching of wrenched rock and of the tearing of the Earth's crust; and then a sickening lurch, a nauseous dip and lunge of sideward motion, a sense of acceleration; and then a howling sound, the howling of a sudden, tremendous wind. The generals were all thrown to the floor, trembling.

Somehow the physicist had remained standing, holding the sides of the table on which his instruments were mounted. His old hands were white with the strain and were trembling, but his face was ecstatic. 'Amazing!' he said. 'Amazing!' His eyes were shining.

'What happened?' one of the generals said weakly, from the floor.

'Propkofski! Propkofski was right!' said the other, his voice jubilant, shaking with emotion. 'That *was* the intersection of the mass-influx lines. The brick, the gold brick, was the keystone, the hub! It held the Earth up.'

'What,' said the general, shouting above the roar of the wind that was now like a cyclone, above the screeching of twisted rock and the wrenching of the very bowels of the Earth. 'What does that *mean*?'

'It means that Propkofski must have been right!' said the other, his voice quivering. 'The Earth, it seems, is falling into the sun!'

The Ifth of Oofth

Farnsworth had invented a new drink that night. He called it a mulled sloe gin toddy. Exactly as fantastic as it sounds – ramming a red-hot poker into a mugful of warm red gin, cinnamon, cloves and sugar, and then *drinking* the fool thing – but like many of Farnsworth's ideas, it managed somehow to work out. In fact, its flavor had become completely acceptable to me after the third one.

When he finally set the end of his steaming poker back on the coals for regeneration, I leaned back in my big leather chair – the one he had rigged up so that it would gently rock you to sleep if you pressed the right button – and said, 'Oliver, your ingenuity is matched only by your hospitality.'

Farnsworth blushed and smiled. He is a small, chubby man and blushes easily. 'Thank you,' he said. 'I have another new one. I call it a jelled vodka fizz – you eat it with a spoon. You may want to try it later. It's – well – exceptional.'

I suppressed a shudder at the thought of eating jelled vodka and said, 'Interesting, very interesting,' and since he didn't reply, we both stared at the fire for a while, letting the gin continue its pleasant work. Farnsworth's bachelor home was very comfortable and relaxing, and I always enjoyed my Wednesday night visits there thoroughly. I suppose most men have a deep-seated love for open fires and liquor – however fantastically prepared – and leather armchairs.

Then, after several minutes, Farnsworth bounced to his feet and said, 'There's a thing I wanted to show you. Made it last week. Didn't pull it off too well, though.'

'Really?' I said. I'd thought the drinks had been his weekly brainchild. They seemed quite enough.

'Yes,' he said, trotting over to the door of the study.

'It's downstairs in the shop. I'll get it.' And he bounced out of the room, the paneled door closing as it had opened, automatically, behind him.

I turned back to the fire again, pleased that he had made something in the machine shop – the carpentry shop was in a shed in the backyard; the chemistry and optical labs in the attic – for he was at his best with his lathe and milling machines. His self-setting, variable-twist thumb bolt had been a beautiful piece of work and its patent had made him a lot of money.

He returned in a minute, carrying a very odd-looking thing with him, and set it on the table beside my chair. I examined it for a minute while Farnsworth stood over me, half smiling, his little green eyes wide, sparkling in the flickering light from the fire. I knew he was suppressing his eagerness for my comment, but I was unsure what to say.

The thing appeared simple: a cross-shaped construction of several dozen one-inch cubes, half of them of thin, transparent plastic, the other half made of thin little sheets of aluminum. Each cube was hinged to two others very cunningly and the arrangement of them all was confusing.

Finally, I said, 'How many cubes?' I had tried to count them, but kept getting lost.

'Sixty-four,' he said. 'I think.'

'You *think*?'

'Well—' He seemed embarrassed. 'At least I *made* sixty-four cubes, thirty-two of each kind; but somehow I haven't been able to count them since. They seem to . . . get lost, or shift around, or something.'

'Oh?' I was becoming interested. 'May I pick it up?'

'Certainly,' he said, and I took the affair, which was surprisingly lightweight, in my hands and began folding the cubes around on their hinges. I noticed then that some were open on one side and that certain others would fit into these if their hinging arrangements would allow them to.

I began folding them absently and said, 'You could count them by marking them one at a time. With a

41

crayon, for instance.'

'As a matter of fact,' he admitted, blushing again, 'I tried that. Didn't seem to work out. When I finished, I found I had marked six cubes with the number one and on none of them could I find a two or three, although there were two fours, one of them written in reverse and in green.' He hesitated. 'I had used a red marking pencil.' I saw him shudder slightly as he said it, although his voice had been casual-sounding enough. 'I rubbed the numbers off with a damp cloth and didn't . . . try it again.'

'Well,' I said. And then, 'What do you call it?'

'A pentaract.'

He sat back down again in his armchair. 'Of course, that name really isn't accurate. I suppose a pentaract should really be a four-dimensional pentagon, and this is meant to be a picture of a five-dimensional cube.'

'A *picture*?' It didn't look like a picture to me.

'Well, it couldn't *really* have five-dimensionality – length, width, breadth, ifth and oofth – or I don't think it could.' His voice faltered a little at that. 'But it's supposed to illustrate the layout of an object that did have those.'

'What kind of object would that be?' I looked back at the thing in my lap and was surprised to see that I had folded a good many of the cubes together.

'Suppose,' he said, 'you put a lot of points in a row, touching; you have a line – a one-dimensional figure. Put four lines together at right angles and on a plane; a square – two-dimensional. Six squares at right angles and extended into real space give you a cube – three dimensions. And eight cubes extended into four physical dimensions give you a tesseract, as it's called—'

'And eight tesseracts make a pentaract,' I said. 'Five dimensions.'

'Exactly. But naturally this is just a *picture* of a pentaract, in that sense. There probably isn't any ifth and oofth at all.'

'I still don't know what you mean by a *picture*,' I said. pushing the cubes around interestedly.

'You don't?' he asked, pursing his lips. 'It's rather

awkward to explain, but . . . well, on the surface of a piece of paper, you can make a very realistic picture of a cube – you know, with perspective and shading and all that kind of thing – and what you'd actually be doing would be illustrating a three-dimensional object, the cube, by using only two dimensions to do it with.'

'And of course,' I said, 'you could *fold* the paper into a cube. Then you'd have a real cube.'

He nodded. 'But you'd have to *use* the third dimension – by folding the flat paper *up* – to do it. So unless I could fold my cubes up through ifth or oofth, my pentaract will have to be just a poor picture.'

'Well!' I said, a bit lost. 'And what do you plan to use it for?'

'Just curiosity.' And then, abruptly, looking at me now, his eyes grew wide and he bumped up out of his chair. He said breathlessly, 'What have you done to it?'

I looked down at my hands. I was holding a little structure of eight cubes, joined together in a small cross. 'Why, nothing,' I said, feeling a little foolish. 'I only folded most of them together.'

'That's impossible! There were only twelve open ones to begin with! All of the others were six-sided!'

Farnsworth made a grab for it, apparently beside himself; the gesture was so sudden that I drew back. It made Farnsworth miss his grab and the little object flew from my hands and hit the floor, solidly, on one of its corners. There was a slight bump as it hit, and a faint clicking noise, and the thing seemed to crumple in a peculiar way. Sitting in front of us on the floor was a little one-inch cube, and nothing else.

For at least a full minute, we stared at it. Then I stood up and looked in my chair seat, looked around the floor of the room, even got down on my knees and peered under the chair. Farnsworth was watching me, and when I finished and sat down again, he asked, 'No others?'

'No other cubes,' I said, 'anywhere.'

'I was afraid of that.' He pointed an unsteady finger at the one cube in front of us. 'I suppose they're all in there.'

Some of his agitation had begun to wear off and after a moment he said, 'What was that you said about folding the paper to make a cube?'

I looked at him and managed an apologetic smile.

He didn't smile back, but he got up and said, 'Well, I doubt if it can bite,' and bent over and picked the cube up, hefting its weight carefully in his hand. 'It seems to weigh the same as the – sixty-four did,' he said, quite calmly now. Then he looked at it closely and suddenly became agitated again. 'Good heavens! Look at this!' He held it up. On one side, exactly in the center, was a neat little hole, about a half-inch across.

I moved my head closer to the cube and saw that the hole was not really circular. It was like the iris diaphragm of a camera, a polygon made of many overlapping, straight pieces of metal, allowing an opening for light to enter. Nothing was visible through the hole; I could see only an undefined blackness.

'I don't understand how . . .' I began, and stopped.

'Nor I,' he said. 'Let's see if there's anything in here.'

He put the cube up to his eye and squinted and peered for a minute. Then he carefully set it on the table, walked to his chair, sat down and folded his hands over his fat little lap.

'George,' he said, 'there *is* something in there.' His voice now was very steady and yet strange.

'What?' I asked. What else do you say?

'A little ball,' he said. 'A little round ball. Quite misted over, but nonetheless a ball.'

'Well!' I said.

'George, I'll get the gin.'

He was back from the sideboard in what seemed an incredibly short time. He had the sloe gin in highball glasses, with ice and water. It tasted horrible.

When I finished mine, I said, 'Delicious. Let's have another,' and we did. After I drank that one, I felt a good deal more rational.

I set my glass down. 'Farnsworth, it just occurred to me. Isn't the fourth dimension supposed to be *time*, according to Einstein?'

He had finished his second sloe gin highball, unmulled, by then. 'Supposed to be, yes, according to Einstein. I call it ifth – or oofth – take your pick.' He held up the cube again, much more confidently now, I noticed. 'And what about the *fifth* dimension?'

'Beats me,' I said, looking at the cube, which was beginning to seem vaguely sinister to me. 'Beats the hell out of me.'

'Beats me, too, George,' he said almost gaily – an astonishing mood for old Farnsworth. He turned the cube around with his small, fat fingers. 'This is probably all wrapped up in time in some strange way. Not to mention the very peculiar kind of space it appears to be involved with. Extraordinary, don't you think?'

'Extraordinary,' I nodded.

'George, I think I'll take another look.' And he put the cube back to his eye again. 'Well,' he said, after a moment of squinting, 'same little ball.'

'What's it doing?' I wanted to know.

'Nothing. Or perhaps spinning a bit. I'm not sure. It's quite fuzzy, you see, and misty. Dark in there, too.'

'Let me see,' I said, realizing that, after all, if Farnsworth could see the thing in there, so could I.

'In a minute. I wonder what sort of time I'm looking into – past or future, or what?'

'And what sort of space . . .' I was saying when, suddenly, little Farnsworth let out a shriek, dropped the cube as if it had suddenly turned into a snake, and threw his hands over his eyes.

He sank back into his chair and cried, 'My God! My God!'

'What happened?' I asked, rushing over to Farnsworth, who was squirming in his armchair, his face still hidden by his hands.

'My eye!' he moaned, almost sobbing. 'It stabbed my eye! Quick, George, call me an ambulance!'

I hurried to the telephone and fumbled with the book, looking for the right number, until Farnsworth said,

'Quick, George!' again and in desperation, I dialed the operator and told her to send us an ambulance.

When I got back to Farnsworth, he had taken his hand from the unhurt eye and I could see that a trickle of blood was beginning to run down the other wrist. He had almost stopped squirming, but from his face it was obvious that the pain was still intense.

He stood up. 'I need another drink,' he said, and was heading unsteadily for the sideboard when he stepped on the cube, which was still lying in front of his chair, and was barely able to keep himself from falling headlong, tripping on it. The cube skidded a few feet, stopping, hole-side up, near the fire.

He said to the cube, enraged, 'Damn you, I'll show you . . . !' and he reached down and swooped up the poker from the hearth. It had been lying there for mulling drinks, its end resting on the coals, and by now it was a brilliant cherry red. He took the handle with both hands and plunged the red-hot tip into the hole of the cube, pushing it down against the floor.

'I'll show you!' he yelled again, and I watched understandingly as he shoved with all his weight, pushing and twisting, forcing the poker down with angry energy. There was a faint hissing sound and little wisps of dark smoke came from the hole, around the edges of the poker.

Then there was a strange, sucking noise and the poker began to sink into the cube. It must have gone in at least eight or ten inches – impossible, of course, since it was a one-inch cube – and even Farnsworth became so alarmed at this that he yanked the poker out of the hole.

As he did, black smoke arose in a little column for a moment and then there was a popping sound and the cube fell apart, scattering itself into hundreds of squares of plastic and aluminum.

Oddly enough, there were no burn marks on the aluminum and none of the plastic seemed to have melted. There was no sign of a little, misty ball.

Farnsworth returned his right hand to his now puffy and bloody eye. He stood staring at the profusion of little squares with his good eye. His free hand was trembling.

Then there was the sound of a siren, becoming louder. He turned and looked at me balefully. 'That must be the ambulance. I suppose I'd better get my toothbrush.'

Farnsworth lost the eye. Within a week, though, he was pretty much his old chipper self again, looking quite dapper with a black leather patch. One interesting thing – the doctor remarked that there were powder burns of some sort on the eyelid, and that the eye itself appeared to have been destroyed by a small explosion. He assumed that it had been a case of a gun misfiring, the cartridge exploding in an open breech somehow. Farnsworth let him think that; it was as good an explanation as any.

I suggested to Farnsworth that he ought to get a green patch, to match his other eye. He laughed at the idea and said he thought it might be a bit showy. He was already starting work on another pentaract; he was going to find out just what . . .

But he never finished. Nine days after the accident, there was a sudden flurry of news reports from the other side of the world, fantastic stories that made the tabloids go wild, and we began to guess what had happened. There wouldn't be any need to build the sixty-four-cube cross and try to find a way of folding it up. We knew now.

It *had* been a five-dimensional cube, all right. And one extension of it had been in time – into the future; nine days into the future – and the other extension had been into a peculiar kind of space, one that distorted sizes quite strangely.

All of this became obvious when, three days later, it happened on our side of the world and the tabloids were scooped by the phenomenon itself, which, by its nature, required no newspaper reporting.

Across the entire sky of the Western Hemisphere there appeared – so vast that it eclipsed the direct light of the sun from Fairbanks, Alaska, to Cape Horn – a tremendous human eye, with a vast, glistening, green iris. Part of the lid was there, too, and all of it was as if framed in a gigantic circle. Or not exactly a circle, but a polygon of many sides, like the iris diaphragm of a camera shutter.

Toward nightfall, the eye blinked once and probably five hundred million people screamed simultaneously. It remained there all of the night, glowing balefully in the reflected sunlight, obliterating the stars.

Probably more than half the people on Earth thought it was God. Only two knew that it was Oliver Farnsworth, peering at a misty little spinning ball in a five-dimensional box, nine days before, totally unaware that the little ball was the Earth itself, contained in a little one-inch cube that was an enclave of swollen time and shrunken space.

When I had dropped the pentaract and had somehow caused it to fold itself into two new dimensions, it had reached out through fifth-dimensional space and folded the world into itself, and had begun accelerating the time within it, in rough proportion to size, so that as each minute passed in Farnsworth's study, about one day was passing on the world within the cube.

We knew this because about a minute had passed while Farnsworth had held his eye against the cube the second time – the first time had, of course, been the appearance over Asia – and nine days later, when we saw the same event from our position on the Earth in the cube, it was twenty-six hours before the eye was 'stabbed' and withdrew.

It happened early in the morning, just after the sun had left the horizon and was passing into eclipse behind the great circle that contained the eye. Someone stationed along a defense-perimeter station panicked – someone highly placed. Fifty guided missiles were launched, straight up, the most powerful on Earth. Each carried a hydrogen warhead. Even before the great shock wave from their explosion came crashing down to earth, the eye had disappeared.

Somewhere, I knew, an unimaginably vast Oliver Farnsworth was squirming and yelping, carrying out the identical chain of events that I had seen happening in the past and that yet must be happening now, along the immutable space-time continuum that Farnsworth's little cube had somehow by-passed.

The doctor had talked of powder burns. I wondered what he would think if he knew that Farnsworth had been hit in the eye with fifty infinitesimal hydrogen bombs.

For a week, there was nothing else to talk about in the world. Three billion people probably discussed, thought about and dreamed of nothing else. There had been no more dramatic happening since the creation of the earth and sun than the appearance of Farnsworth's eye.

But two people, out of those three billion, thought of something else. They thought of the unchangeable, preset spacetime continuum, moving at the rate of one minute for every day that passed here on our side of the pentaract, while that vast Oliver Farnsworth and I in the other-space, other-time, were staring at the cube that contained our world, lying on their floor.

On Wednesday, we could say, *Now he's gone to the telephone.* On Thursday, *Now he's looking through the book.* On Saturday, *By now he must be dialing the operator* . . .

And on Tuesday morning, when the sun came up, we were together and saw it rise, for we spent our nights together by then, because we did not want to be alone; and when the day had begun, we didn't say it, because we couldn't. But we thought it.

We thought of a colossal, cosmic Farnsworth saying, 'I'll show you!' and shoving, pushing and twisting, forcing with all of his might, into the little round hole, a brilliantly glowing, hissing, smoking, red-hot poker.

The Scholar's Disciple

He appeared to be no more than twenty-five, and his eyes were bright orange. Except for these he would have looked like an ordinary, somewhat handsome young man. He stood in the center of the chalked diagram on Webley's kitchen linoleum and shifted his weight from one small foot to the other. He was dressed impeccably in an Oxford gray suit and he wore a 'peace' button in his lapel.

Webley sat motionless on the kitchen stool for a moment, not knowing exactly what to say. This sort of . . . person was not at all what he had expected. His guest glanced uneasily at the two plastic mixing bowls that sat just inside the chalked lines. Finally he blinked his orange eyes and looked at Webley.

'Well?' Webley said.

'Yes sir?' The fellow's voice was polite; it had the controlled tone of a proper young graduate student's.

Webley cleared his throat. 'Aren't you going to drink the blood?' he said, 'or do something with the entrails?'

The other shuddered. 'No, sir.'

Webley began to feel irritated; it had taken a great deal of work to gather the things. 'Then why in Heaven's name are they in the . . . invocation?'

'In whose name, sir?' The young fellow blushed, averting his eyes.

'Sorry. In the name of Hell, then.'

'Yes.' The fellow smiled engagingly and, more at ease, withdrew a bright red cigarette case from his pocket, offering one to his host, who declined it. The cigarettes were long, and coal black. 'I don't really know, sir, why some versions of the procedure call for such things as . . .' he glanced hesitatingly toward the bowls again, 'those. Impure texts, possibly. It's all in the words. One has to say them right. Apparently you mastered the feat well.' He pressed the end of a well-manicured forefinger against the tip of his cigarette and it lit in a tiny burst of flame. When he exhaled, the smoke had a perfumed odor.

Webley was somewhat placated by the compliment, although it had taken a year of searching to dig up those 'impure texts.' 'Well,' he said, 'you *are* a demon, anyway, aren't you?'

'Oh, hell yes,' the fellow said, with feeling. 'By all means.'

'And your name?'

'Makuka . . . It's hard to pronounce, sir . . . Maku-kabuzzeeliam. In Hell our clients generally call me Robert.'

'And you can serve me?'

'After a fashion, yes. Of course, I have a good many other duties.'

Webley poured himself a drink, offering one to the demon, who refused. 'I don't think I would overwork you, Robert. What I want you to do, primarily, is to write a dissertation for me. And, perhaps, a few scholarly articles.'

The demon seemed to think this over a moment. Then he said, 'What field, sir?'

'English. English literature.'

The demon smiled abruptly, revealing even, white teeth. 'That might be interesting, sir,' he said. 'We have a good many of your English writers . . . available, so to speak.' His orange eyes seemed to twinkle. 'And a fine bunch too, sir, I might add. But why,' he said, 'would you ever call up a demon to write your dissertation for you?'

'Well,' Webley said, 'I am one of the few people who know how; that's one consideration. I have my first PhD in Folklore, you see. Done a lot of research in Folklore. After twelve years of it I began to realize that most of the lore worked out very well. I cure a little asthma here and there, with black-eyed peas, practice a little Voodoo – nothing important, just to amuse my friends.'

'Voodoo never has been very effective,' Robert said

51

understandingly. 'Overrated.'

'I fear so. Anyway, I began to realize that I'd never get anywhere in the academic world with a Folklore degree – just isn't recognized by enough schools. The logical thing was to get into a parallel but more respected field. And, with a few good articles, I might be able to swing a professorship.' Webley finished his drink and shuffled, ponderously, over to the sink, where he began fixing another. 'Trouble is, Robert, I hate writing – especially scholarly writing. Consequently, I thought I'd try invoking a demon to do it for me.' He settled back in his chair, smiling, and began sipping the drink. 'I think it's going to work out very well.'

The demon smiled engagingly. 'I hope so,' he said. 'I'll go check with the legal department – about a contract.' He blinked his eyes and vanished . . .

When Robert returned, after more than an hour, he had with him an estimate on the value of Webley's immortal soul. They haggled for a good while before agreeing on the terms, but Webley was quite pleased with them; he had done better than he had expected to. The young demon seemed to bluff very easily.

Webley would, of course, go to Hell upon his death; but he would have a suite there, a mistress – tó be changed yearly – air conditioning – Robert tried to explain to him that Hell was not in the least bit hot; but Webley stuck to his guns on this point – weekly valet service, and ready access to his landlord should any inconvenience develop. He would be roasted over the coals for one day out of every month; but he was guaranteed that there would be no harmful aftereffects from this. 'In fact,' Robert said, 'some of our clients look forward to that part of the life in Hell, since the possibilities for pain among the dead are so few, and the senses are so dulled by the extraordinary amount of pleasure we have to offer.'

'Then why do you have this roasting business at all, if Hell is such a pleasant place?' Webley asked, pouring himself a drink.

'Well, we are under orders from the opposition. We

can't make Him out to be a liar, you know. And then those coals *are* rather unpleasant.'

'I see. But what, then, do they do in Heaven?'

Robert thought a moment. 'It's been a long time since I was there, of course. They sing, mostly, I think. And do exercises or something.'

In return for his agreeing to the damnation Webley would receive the services of Robert for one year, in which time an acceptable dissertation must be written, as well as at least ten publishable scholarly articles. Webley had with him a razor blade to open a vein for signing the contract; he was mildly piqued when the demon brought out a ball point pen, even though the ink was bright red. It dried brown, however.

Immediately after he finished signing there came the sound of a small and dry little voice, from somewhere, it seemed, in the basement. The voice said one word, which it enunciated with precision. '*Agreed.*'

'Who the devil is *that*?' Webley said.

Robert blushed again, momentarily. 'Our . . . legal department, sir,' he said. He folded the contract and then vanished gently . . .

He appeared for work the next morning. Webley had already prepared an office for him in a disused upstairs bedroom, complete with typewriter, *The MLA Style Sheet*, and a small library of learned journals. He worked methodically and well, seemed to take a certain pleasure in his writing, and within three months had produced a monumental, definitive work, titled 'The Lyric Cry in Colley Cibber: A Reappraisal.' When this was finished, Robert suggested that he show it to Mr Cibber, who, he said, had a small walk-up apartment in suburban Hell; but Webley would not hear of it. 'Just stick to the scholarship, young man.'

The dissertation, upon acceptance and publication by the University press, created a stir among a great many academic people, few of whom read it. Webley soon found himself in possession of a very congenial job, with a low salary and few duties. A month later he received a large fellowship from a foundation; and upon his first PMLA publication, the controversy-stirring article 'Threads of Francophilism in John Webster's *The White Devil*,' found himself with an associate professorship and even fewer duties.

The demon's work was inspired. His style managed to be ornate and terse at one and the same time; he was greatly sardonic about everyone and everything except a handful of third-rate poets; he displayed an astonishing prowess at ignoring the obvious and seizing upon the manifestly impossible; and his footnotes were awe-inspiring. Within a year Webley's name had become an unshakeable star in the academic firmament.

When Robert handed the tenth paper to his employer he seemed actually sad that this would be the last of his scholarly work. He had grown to love his job.

Webley, interpreting Robert's hesitancy rightly, was immediately struck by an idea. He explained it to the demon. He, Webley, would apply for a year's leave of absence with pay, so that he might write a book. He had been feeling oppressed, of late, by the restrictions of his teaching schedule, however light; and, besides, there was a graduate assistant, a certain Miss Hopkins, with whom he was much taken. Miss Hopkins had already expressed a deep-seated wish to visit Acapulco. As for himself, he enjoyed spear fishing as well as the next fellow. Now, as for the book . . . He would be glad to sign a new contract.

Robert's face showed doubt, although Webley could tell that he was pleased with the idea. 'I don't know, sir,' he said, 'I do have my other duties; and my supervisor doesn't generally like to alter a contract. People are always accusing him of coercion when he does something like that. He's very scrupulous, you know.'

'Well, see what you can do,' Webley said. 'And remember, you can write the book any way you want to.'

'Well . . .'

'You can name your own subject.'

The demon smiled sheepishly, 'I'll see what I can do,' he

said, and vanished in a puff of perfumed smoke.

It was three days later that Robert returned with the new contract. The terms were fairly hard, but this time Webley was unable to talk them down. Robert said that this was the least his legal department would allow. There would now be three days per month on the coals, together with one day of boils, from sole to crown. Also he would have to share the bath in his suite, and his choice of mistresses would be limited to brunettes. But, in return, Robert promised to produce the finest, most significant and monumental work of English literary criticism ever written.

After four hours of bickering, Webley finally threw his hands in the air. 'All right,' he said, 'I'll sign. After all, a man ought to produce one good book in a lifetime. And Miss Hopkins is growing impatient.'

Robert smiled. 'I'm certain you won't be disappointed in the book, sir.' He blushed slightly. 'Nor in Miss Hopkins either. I took the liberty of checking on her file, and found her . . . promising.'

'That's interesting . . .' Webley said, smiling thoughtfully and taking the ball point pen from the demon's outstretched hand.

As before, there came the little voice, saying, 'Agreed . . .'

Miss Hopkins was not disappointing, not in the least. Nor was Acapulco, nor spear fishing, nor tequila. But especially not Miss Hopkins. When the year ended and Robert appeared, Webley was lying in bed in a small adobe hut, with a mild headache and with Miss Hopkins, who was fortunately sound asleep. The demon, appearing from Hell with a very thick book under his arm, found him there.

During the past year Webley's face had taken on a certain bloated haughtiness; and his tone now with Robert was patronizing. 'What's the title, Robert?' he said, making no move to get up from the bed.

'*The English Literary Tradition: A Re-evaluation.*' There was a tiny hint of pride in Robert's voice.

Webley frowned. 'That's a little general, Robert,' he said. 'But I suppose it'll do. How long is it?'

'Seventeen hundred pages, sir.'

'Yes. Well, that ought to impress them well enough.' He leaned over on one elbow. 'Tell you what you do, Robert. You pack that manuscript off to my editor for me; and then I want you to take a message to the University. Tell them I'm delayed and won't be back for about three or four weeks. Tell them I'm working on the index or something.' He reached a chubby hand over and gave Miss Hopkins a gentle pat on the rump. She stirred and giggled softly in her sleep. 'Now do that for me, Robert, and it'll be all wrapped up between us.'

There seemed to be a hurt look in the demon's eyes. 'You're not going to read the book, sir?'

Webley waved a hand royally. 'When it comes out in print, man,' he said. 'Right now I'm busy.'

'Yes, sir,' Robert said, vanishing.

It was six weeks later that Webley was mailed a copy of the book by his publisher. Since he was well absorbed at the time with other pursuits, it was another two weeks before he read it. Or he did not read it exactly – not entirely. He was two-thirds of the way through when, red in the face and eyes glaring, he shrieked the proper incantation and Robert appeared.

'What in the name of Hell do you mean by this – this asininity, this patent absurdity?' Webley said. 'Any half-baked scholar with a quarter of a brain could demolish this, rip it to shreds! This is tripe, Robert. Fraudulent, unscholarly, unforgivable tripe. You've made an ass of yourself and of me.'

Robert seemed dumbfounded; his entire face was an enormous blush. 'But, Professor Webley,' he said, 'I . . . I thought you would like it, sir. Thought it would be . . . just the thing.'

Webley seemed to explode. 'Just the thing!' He slammed the book on his desk. 'Good lord, Robert, if I couldn't write a more accurate work of literary criticism in six months' time I'd . . . I'd let you roast me in Hell. Seven days a week.'

From somewhere beneath the floor came a little voice, saying 'Agreed.'

Webley stopped in the middle of a breath. Then he said, 'Now wait a minute, Robert. You can't . . . surely you . . .'

The demon's face showed embarrassment, and his tone was extremely polite, apologetic. 'I'm afraid we can, sir,' he said. 'Verbal contract, you know. Hold up in any court.'

For a moment Webley's eyes searched frantically around the room. Finally they landed on the book, which lay now on the table, and immediately the glance of uncertainty was replaced with a look of triumph. 'All right,' he said. 'All right. You think you've got me, don't you? Think you've trapped me into a bad contract. The only thing you've neglected is that I *can* write a better book than this one.' He picked up the book, flipping through it again, 'Look at this. More than two hundred pages of Shakespeare analysis – not to mention the rest, from The Pearl Poet to Oscar Wilde – and not one genuine, scholarly idea in the lot. Well written, possibly. But any graduate student knows that Shakespeare didn't model Cleopatra on his *mother* – the idea's absurd. And an idiot would know that the textual problem is the only clue to *Hamlet*.'

'But . . .' Robert said.

'But nothing!' Webley slammed the book back on his desk. 'It's not merely your insidious way of trying to steal my soul that infuriates me – it's this fool book you're trying to do it with. Who in Hell ever gave you these stupid notions about literature?'

Robert seemed uneasy. 'That's what I've been trying to tell you, Mr Webley,' he said. 'It was a great many people in Hell. You see, I didn't exactly write the book myself, sir.'

'Then who . . . who wrote this nonsense about Shakespeare?'

57

'Shakespeare, sir. I sobered him up and . . .'

Abruptly, Webley's voice took on the tone of a small man speaking from the bottom of a well. 'And Milton. Who . . . ?'

The demon managed a weak smile. 'John had some revealing things to say about *Comus*, didn't he, sir?'

Webley's eyes were taking on a strange, hunted look. 'And *Beowulf* . . . Surely you didn't . . .'

'I'm afraid I did, Mr Webley. We have the author of that one too – he slipped up once on the Fourth Commandment. Fellow named Seothang the Imbiber. Drinks mead.'

Webley stood in stony silence for several minutes, holding the heavy book in a limp hand. His eyes were closed.

After a few minutes he opened them. Robert had, tastefully, vanished. In his place was a small, black table. On this were arranged neatly a typewriter, a stack of white paper, and a calendar.

Far From Home

The first inkling the janitor had of the miracle was the smell of it. This was a small miracle in itself: the salt smell of kelp and seawater in the Arizona morning air. He had just unlocked the front entrance and walked into the building when the smell hit him. Now this man was old and normally did not trust his senses very well; but there was no mistaking this, not even in this most inland of inland towns: it was the smell of ocean – deep ocean, far out, the ocean of green water, kelp and brine.

And strangely, because the janitor was old and tired and because this was the part of early morning that seems unreal to many old men, the first thing the smell made him feel was a small, almost undetectable thrilling in his old nerves, a memory deeper than blood of a time fifty years before when he had gone once, as a boy, to San Francisco and had watched the ships in the bay and had discovered the fine old dirty smell of seawater. But this feeling lasted only an instant. It was replaced immediately with amazement – and then anger, although it would have been impossible to say with what he was angry, here in this desert town, in the dressing rooms of the large public swimming pool at morning, being reminded of his youth and of the ocean.

'What the hell's going on here . . .?' the janitor said.

There was no one to hear this, except perhaps the small boy who had been standing outside, staring through the wire fence into the pool and clutching a brown paper sack in one grubby hand, when the janitor had come up to the building. The man had paid no attention to the boy; small boys were always around the swimming pool in summer – a nuisance. The boy, if he had heard the man, did not reply.

The janitor walked on through the concrete-floored

59

dressing rooms, not even stopping to read the morning's crop of obscenities scribbled on the walls of the little wooden booths. He walked into the tiled anteroom, stepped across the disinfectant foot bath, and out onto the wide concrete edge of the swimming pool itself.

Some things are unmistakable. There was a whale in the pool.

And no ordinary, everyday whale. This was a monumental creature, a whale's whale, a great, blue-gray leviathan, ninety feet long and thirty feet across the back, with a tail the size of a flatcar and a head like the smooth fist of a titan. A blue whale, an old shiny, leathery monster with barnacles on his gray underbelly and his eyes filmed with age and wisdom and myopia, with brown seaweed dribbling from one corner of his mouth, marks of the suckers in the unconscious blubber of his back. He rested on his belly in the pool, his back way out of the water and with his monstrous gray lips together in an expression of contentment and repose. He was not asleep; but he was asleep enough not to care where he was.

And he stank – with the fine old stink of the sea, the mother of us all: the brackish, barnacled, grainy salt stink of creation and old age, the stink of the world that was and of the world to come. He was beautiful.

The janitor did not freeze when he saw him; he froze a moment afterward. First he said, aloud, his voice matter-of-fact, 'There's a whale in the swimming pool. A goddamn whale.' He said this to no one – or to everyone – and perhaps the boy heard him, although there was no reply from the other side of the fence.

After speaking, the janitor stood where he was for seven minutes, thinking. He thought of many things, such as what he had eaten for breakfast, what his wife had said to him when she had awakened him that morning. Somewhere, in the corner of his vision, he saw the little boy with the paper sack, and his mind thought, as minds will do at such times, *Now that boy's about six years old. That's probably his lunch in that sack. Egg salad sandwich*

Banana. Or apple. But he did not think about the whale, because there was nothing to be thought about the whale. He stared at its unbelievable bulk, resting calmly, the great head in the deep water under the diving boards, the corner of one tail fluke being lapped gently by the shallow water of the wading pool.

The whale breathed slowly, deeply, through its blow hole. The janitor breathed slowly, shallowly, staring, not blinking even in the rising sunlight, staring with no comprehension at the eighty-five-ton miracle in the swimming pool. The boy held his paper sack tightly at the top, and his eyes, too, remained fixed on the whale. The sun was rising in the sky over the desert to the east, and its light glinted in red and purple iridescence on the oily back of the whale.

And then the whale noticed the janitor. Weak-visioned, it peered at him filmily for several moments from its grotesquely small eye. And then it arched its back in a ponderous, awesome, and graceful movement, lifted its tail twenty feet in the air, and brought it down in a way that seemed strangely slow, slapping gently into the water with it. A hundred gallons of water rose out of the pool, and enough of it drenched the janitor to wake him from the state of partial paralysis into which he had fallen.

Abruptly the janitor jumped back, scrambling from the water, his eyes looking, frightened, in all directions, his lips white. There was nothing to see but the whale and the boy. 'All right,' he said. 'All right,' as if he had somehow seen through the plot, as if he knew, now, what a whale would be doing in the public swimming pool, as if no one was going to put anything over on *him*. 'All right,' the janitor said to the whale, and then he turned and ran.

He ran back into the center of town, back toward Main Street, back toward the bank, where he would find the Chairman of the Board of the City Parks Commission, the man who could, somehow – perhaps with a memorandum – save him. He ran back to the town where things were as they were supposed to be; ran as fast as he had ever run,

61

even when young, to escape the only miracle he would ever see in his life and the greatest of all God's creatures . . .

After the janitor had left, the boy remained staring at the whale for a long while, his face a mask and his heart racing with all the peculiar excitement of wonder and love – wonder for all whales, and love for the only whale that he, an Arizona boy of six desert years, had ever seen. And then, when he realized that there would be men there soon and his time with his whale would be over, he lifted the paper sack carefully close to his face, and opened its top about an inch. A commotion began in the sack, as if a small animal were in it that wanted desperately to get out.

'Stop that!' the boy said, frowning.

The kicking stopped. From the sack came a voice – a highpitched, irascible voice. 'All right, whatever-your-name-is,' the voice said, 'I suppose you're ready for the second one.'

The boy held the sack carefully with his thumb and forefinger. He frowned at the opening in the top. 'Yes,' he said, 'I think so . . .'

When the janitor returned with the two other men, the whale was no longer there. Neither was the small boy. But the seaweed smell and the splashed, brackish water were there still, and in the pool were several brownish streamers of seaweed, floating aimlessly in the chlorinated water, far from home.

PART TWO
Close to Home

Rent Control

'My God,' Edith said, 'that was the most *real* experience of my life.' She put her arms around him, put her cheek against his naked chest, and pulled him tightly to her. She was crying.

He was crying too. 'Me too, darling,' he said, and held his arms around her. They were in the loft bed of her studio apartment on the East Side. They had just had orgasms together. Now they were sweaty, relaxed, blissful. It had been a perfect day.

Their orgasms had been foreshadowed by their therapy. That evening, after supper, they had gone to Harry's group as always on Wednesdays and somehow everything had focused for them. He had at last shouted the heartfelt anger he bore against his incompetent parents; she had screamed her hatred of her sadistic mother, her gutless father. And their relief had come together there on the floor of a New York psychiatrist's office. After the screaming and pounding of fists, after the real and potent old rage in both of them was spent, their smiles at one another had been radiant. They had gone afterward to her apartment, where they had lived together half a year, climbed up the ladder into her bed, and begun to make love slowly, carefully. Then frenetically. They had been picked up bodily by it and carried to a place they had never been before.

Now, afterward, they were settling down in that place, huddled together. They lay silently for a long time. Idly he looked toward the ledge by the mattress where she kept cigarettes, a mason jar with miniature roses, a Japanese ashtray, and an alarm clock.

'The clock must have stopped,' she said.

He mumbled something inarticulate. His eyes were closed.

'It says nine twenty,' she said, 'and we left Harry's at nine.'

'Hmmm,' he said, without interest.

She was silent for a while, musing then she said, 'Terry? What time does your watch say?'

'Time, time.' he said. 'Watch, watch.' He shifted his arm and looked. 'Nine twenty,' he said.

'Is the second hand moving?' she said. His watch was an Accutron, not given to being wrong or stopping.

He looked again. 'Nope. Not moving.' He let his hand fall on her naked behind, now cool to his touch. Then he said, 'That *is* funny. Both stopping at once.' He leaned over her body toward the window, pried open a space in her Levelor blinds, looked out. It was dark out, with an odd shimmer to the air. Nothing was moving. There was a pile of plastic garbage bags on the sidewalk opposite. 'It can't be eleven yet. They haven't taken the garbage from the Toreador.' The Toreador was a Spanish restaurant across the street; they kept promising they would eat there sometime but never had.

'It's probably about ten thirty,' she said. 'Why don't you make us an omelet and turn the TV on?'

'Sure, honey,' he said. He slipped on his bikini shorts and eased himself down the ladder. Barefoot and undressed, he went to the tiny Sony by the fireplace, turned it on, and padded over to the stove and sink at the other end of the room. He heard the TV come on while finding the omelet pan that he had bought her, under the sink, nestling between the Bon Ami and the Windex. He got eggs out, cracked one, looked at his watch. It was running. It said nine twenty-six. 'Hey, honey,' he called out. 'My watch is running.'

After a pause she said, her voice slightly hushed, 'So is the clock up here.'

He shrugged and put butter in the pan and finished cracking the eggs, throwing the shells into the sink. He whipped them with a fork, then turned on the fire under the pan and walked back to the TV for a moment. A voice was saying, '. . . nine thirty.' He looked at his watch. Nine

66

thirty. '*Jesus Christ*!' he said.

But he had forgotten about it by the time he cooked the omelets. His omelets had been from the beginning one of the things that made them close. He had learned to cook them before leaving his wife and it meant independence to him. He made omelets beautifully – tender and moist – and Edith was impressed. They had fallen in love over omelets. He cooked lamb chops too, and bought things like frozen capelletti from expensive shops; but omelets were central.

They were both thirty-five years old, both youthful, good-looking, smart. They were both Pisces, with birthdays three days apart. Both had good complexions, healthy dark hair, clear eyes. They both bought clothes at Bergdorf-Goodman and Bonwit's and Bloomingdale's; they both spoke fair French, watched *Nova* on TV, read *The Stories of John Cheever* and the Sunday *Times*. He was a magazine illustrator, she a lawyer; they could have afforded a bigger place, but hers was rent-controlled and at a terrific midtown address. It was too much of a bargain to give up. '*Nobody* ever leaves a rent-controlled apartment,' she told him. So they lived in one and a half rooms together and money piled up in their bank accounts.

They were terribly nervous lovers at first, too unsure of everything to enjoy it, full of explanations and self-recriminations. He had trouble staying hard; she would not lubricate. She was afraid of him and made love dutifully, often with resentment. He was embarrassed at his unreliable member, sensed her withdrawal from his ardor, was afraid to tell her so. Often they were miserable.

But she had the good sense to take him to her therapist and he had the good sense to go. Finally, after six months of private sessions and of group, it had worked. They had the perfect orgasm, the perfect release from tension, the perfect intimacy.

Now they ate their omelets in bed from Spode plates, using his mother's silver forks. Sea salt and Java pepper. Their legs were twined as they ate.

67

They lay silent for a while afterward. He looked out the window. The garbage was still there; there was no movement in the street; no one was on the sidewalk. There was a flatness to the way the light shone on the buildings across from them, as though they were painted – some kind of a backdrop.

He looked at his watch. It said nine forty-one. The second hand wasn't moving. 'Shit!' he said, puzzled.

'What's that, honey?' Edith said. 'Did I do something wrong?'

'No, sweetie,' he said. 'You're the best thing that ever happened. I'm crazy about you.' He patted her ass with one hand, gave her his empty plate with the other.

She set the two plates on the ledge, which was barely wide enough for them. She glanced at the clock. 'Jesus,' she said. 'That sure is strange . . .'

'Let's go to sleep,' he said. 'I'll explain the Theory of Relativity in the morning.'

But when he woke up it wasn't morning. He felt refreshed, thoroughly rested; he had the sense of a long and absolutely silent sleep, with no noises intruding from the world outside, no dreams, no complications. He had never felt better.

But when he looked out the window the light from the streetlamp was the same and the garbage bags were still piled in front of the Toreador and – he saw now – what appeared to be the same taxi was motionless in front of the same green station wagon in the middle of Fifty-first Street. He looked at his watch. It said nine forty-one.

Edith was still asleep, on her stomach, with her arm across his waist, her hip against his. Not waking her, he pulled away and started to climb down from the bed. On an impulse he looked again at his watch. It was nine forty-one still, but now the second hand was moving.

He reached out and turned the electric clock on the ledge to where he could see its face. It said nine forty-one also, and when he held it to his ear he could hear its gears turning quietly inside. His heart began to beat more strongly, and he found himself catching his breath.

He climbed down and went to the television set, turned it on again. The same face appeared as before he had slept, wearing the same oversized glasses, the same bland smile.

Terry turned the sound up, seated himself on the sofa, lit a cigarette, and waited.

It seemed a long time before the news program ended and a voice said, 'It's ten o'clock.'

He looked at his watch. It said ten o'clock. He looked out the window; it was dark – evening. There was no way it could be ten in the morning. But he knew he had slept a whole night. He knew it. His hand holding the second cigarette was trembling.

Slowly and carefully he put out his cigarette, climbed back up the ladder to the loft bed. Edith was still asleep. Somehow he knew what to do. He laid his hand on her leg and looked at his watch. As he touched her the second hand stopped. For a long moment he did not breathe.

Still holding her leg, he looked out the window. This time there were a group of people outside; they had just left the restaurant. None of them moved. The taxi had gone and with it the station wagon; but the garbage was still there. One of the people from the Toreador was in the process of putting on his raincoat. One arm was in a sleeve and the other wasn't. There was a frown on his face visible from the third-story apartment where Terry lay looking at him. Everything was frozen. The light was peculiar, unreal. The man's frown did not change.

Terry let go of Edith and the man finished putting on his coat. Two cars drove by in the street. The light became normal.

Terry touched Edith again, this time laying his hand gently on her bare back. Outside the window everything stopped, as when a switch is thrown on a projector to arrest the movement. Terry let out his breath audibly. Then he said, 'Wake up, Edith. I've got something to show you.'

69

They never understood it, and they told nobody. It was relativity, they decided. They had found, indeed, a perfect place together, where subjective time raced and the world did not.

It did not work anywhere but in her loft bed and only when they touched. They could stay together there for hours or days, although there was no way they could tell how long the 'time' had really been; they could make love, sleep, read, talk, and no time passed whatever.

They discovered, after a while, that only if they quarreled did it fail and the clock and watch would run even though they were touching. It required intimacy – even of a slight kind, the intimacy of casual touching – for it to work.

They adapted their lives to it quickly and at first it extended their sense of life's possibilities enormously. It bathed them in a perfection of the lovers' sense of being apart from the rest of the world and better than it. ·

Their careers improved; they had more time for work and for play than anyone else. If one of them was ever under serious pressure – of job competition, of the need to make a quick decision – they could get in bed together and have all the time necessary to decide, to think up the speech, to plan the magazine cover or the case in court.

Sometimes they took what they called 'weekends,' buying and cooking enough food for five or six meals, and just staying in the loft bed, touching, while reading and meditating and making love and working. He had his art supplies in shelves over the bed now, and she had reference books and note pads on the ledge. He had put mirrors on two of the walls and on the ceiling, partly for sex, partly to make the small place seem bigger, less confining.

The food was always hot, unspoiled; no time had passed for it between their meals. They could not watch television or listen to records while in suspended time; no machinery worked while they touched.

Sometimes for fun they would watch people out the window and stop and start them up again comically; but window and stop and start them up again comically; but that soon grew tiresome.

They both got richer and richer, with promotions and higher pay and the low rent. And of course there was now truly no question of leaving the apartment; there was no other bed in which they could stop time, no other place. Besides, this one was rent-controlled.

For a year or so they would always stay later at parties than anyone else, would taunt acquaintances and colleagues when they were too tired to accompany them to all-night places for scrambled eggs or a final drink. Sometimes they annoyed colleagues by showing up bright-eyed and rested in the morning, no matter how late the party had gone on, no matter how many drinks had been drunk, no matter how loud and fatiguing the revelry. They were always buoyant, healthy, awake, and just a bit smug.

But after the first year they tired of partying, grew bored with friends, and went out less. Somehow they had come to a place where they were never bored with, as Edith called it, 'our little loft bed.' The center of their lives had become a king-sized foam mattress with a foot-wide ledge and a few inches of head and foot room at each end. They were never bored when in that small space.

What they had to learn was not to quarrel, not to lose the modicum of intimacy that their relativity phenomenon required. But that came easily too; without discussing it each learned to give only a small part of himself to intimacy with the other, to cultivate a state of mind remote enough to be safe from conflict, yet with a controlled closeness. They did yoga for body and spirit and Transcendental Meditation. Neither told the other his mantra. Often they found themselves staring at different mirrors. Now they seldom looked out the window.

It was Edith who made the second major intuition. One day when he was in the bathroom shaving, and his watch was running, he heard her shout at him, in a kind of cool

71

playfulness, 'Quit dawdling in there, Terry. I'm getting older for nothing.' There was some kind of urgency in her voice, and he caught it. He rinsed his face off in a hurry, dried, walked to the bedroom and looked up at her. 'What do you mean?' he said.

She didn't look at him. 'Get on up here, Dum-dum,' she said, still in that controlled-playful voice. 'I want you to touch me.'

He climbed up, laid a hand on her shoulder. Outside the window a walking man froze in mid-stride and the sunlight darkened as though a shutter had been placed over it.

'What do you mean, "older for nothing"?' he said.

She looked at him thoughtfully. 'It's been about five years now, in the real world,' she said. 'The real world' for them meant the time lived by other people. 'But we must have spent five years in suspended time here in bed. More than that. And we haven't been aged by it.'

He looked at her. 'How could . . . ?'

'I don't know,' she said. 'But I know we're not any older than anybody else.'

He turned toward the mirror at her feet, stared at himself in it. He was still youthful, firm, clear complexioned. Suddenly he smiled at himself. 'Jesus,' he said. 'Maybe I can fix it so I can shave in bed.'

Their 'weekends' became longer. Although they could not measure their special time, the number of times they slept and the times they made love could be counted; and both those numbers increased once they realized the time in bed together was 'free' – that they did not age while touching, in the loft bed, while the world outside was motionless and the sun neither rose nor set.

Sometimes they would pick a time of day and a quality of light they both liked and stop their time there. At twilight, with empty streets and a soft ambience of light, they would allow for the slight darkening effect, and then touch and stay touching for eight or ten sleeping periods, six or eight orgasms, fifteen meals.

They had stopped the omelets because of the real time it took to prepare them. Now they bought pizzas and prepared chickens and ready-made desserts and quarts of milk and coffee and bottles of good wine and cartons of cigarettes and cases of Perrier water and filled shelves at each side of the window with them. The hot food would never cool as long as Edith and Terry were touching each other in the controlled intimacy they now had learned as second nature. Each could look at himself in his own mirror and not even think about the other in a conscious way, but if their fingertips were so much as touching and if the remote sense of the other was unruffled by anger or anxiety then the pizzas on the shelf would remain hot, the Perrier cold, the cars in the street motionless, and the sky and weather without change forever. No love was needed now, no feeling whatever – only the lack of unpleasantness and the slightest of physical contact.

The world outside became less interesting for them. They both had large bank accounts and both had good yet undemanding jobs; her legal briefs were prepared by assistants; three young men in his studio made the illustrations that he designed, on drawing pads, in the loft bed. Often the nights were a terrible bore to them when they had to let go of each other if they wanted morning to come, just so they could go to work, have a change of pace.

But less and less did either of them want the pace to change. Each had learned to spend 'hours' motionless, staring at the mirror or out the window, preserving his youth against the ravages of real time and real movement. Each became obsessed, without sharing the obsession, with a single idea: immortality. They could live forever, young and healthy and fully awake, in this loft bed. There was no question of interestingness or of boredom; they had moved, deeply in their separate souls, far beyond that distinction, the rhythm of life. Deep in themselves they had become a Pharaoh's dream of endless time; they had found the pyramid that kept the flow of the world away.

On one autumn morning that had been like two weeks for them he looked at her, after waking, and said, 'I don't want to leave this place. I don't want to get old.'

She looked at him before she spoke. Then she said, 'There's nothing I want to do outside.'

He looked away from her, smiling. 'We'll need a lot of food,' he said.

They had already had the apartment filled with shelves and a bathroom was installed beneath the bed. Using the bathroom was the only concession to real time; to make the water flow it was necessary for them not to touch.

They filled the shelves, that autumn afternoon, with hundreds of pounds of food – cheeses and hot chickens and sausage and milk and butter and big loaves of bread and precooked steaks and pork chops and hams and bowls of cooked vegetables, all prepared and delivered by a wondering caterer and five assistants. They had cases of wine and beer and cigarettes. It was like an efficient, miniature warehouse.

When they got into bed and touched she said, 'What if we quarrel? The food will all spoil.'

'I know,' he said. And then, taking a deep breath, 'What if we just don't talk?'

She looked at him for a long moment. Then she said, 'I've been thinking that too.'

So they stopped talking. And each turned toward his own mirror and thought of living forever. They were back to back, touching.

No friend found them, for they had no friends. But when the landlord came in through the empty shelves on what was for him the next day he found them in the loft bed, back to back, each staring into a different mirror. They were perfectly beautiful, with healthy, clear complexions, youthful figures, dark and glistening hair; but they had no

74

minds at all. They were not even like beautiful children; there was nothing there but prettiness.

The landlord was shocked at what he saw. But he recognized soon afterward that they would be sent somewhere and that he would be able to charge a profitable rent, at last, with someone new.

A Visit From Mother

(for Herry O. Teltcher)

By the marble fireplace in the main bedroom a discreet
television set was playing. It sat on a Regency stool with
inlaid legs. The program was a videotape of a ballet.

'My God,' Mother said, as he brought her and Daddy
in. 'It's in *color*!'

Barney was flustered. They had been dead a dozen
years and for a moment he had forgotten. 'Sure, Mom,' he
said. 'Color TV's been around for years . . .'

Mother's face, bright for a moment, became wistful.
'It's a pity,' she said. 'Your father would have enjoyed it
so . . .'

Barney glanced at his father shyly, then glanced away.
His father's face was impassive; as always, he neither
confirmed nor denied what Mother had said about him.

'Would you like something to drink?' Barney said to
her. 'Coffee maybe?' It was eleven in the morning.

'You go ahead, Barney,' Mother said, pronouncing his
name with a kind of sigh. 'I don't want anything for
myself.'

She was wearing the same J. C. Penney dress she had
worn to Daddy's funeral, the same black patent shoes.
Daddy was wearing a blue serge Nixon suit and brown
shoes. His hair was pale gray; his face was pained, as
though his false teeth were hurting.

They were both Midwesterners and they looked out of
place in this New York apartment. Somehow, Barney
remembered, they had even looked out of place in their
own Ohio ranch house, however much Mother had tried
to possess the space of it by endless dusting of furniture,
by the covering of its cheap parquet floors with her own
hooked rugs. Daddy alone had filled and held one corner
of the living room of that airless house with its pastel

76

walls, its Currier and Ives prints, the hooked rugs everywhere, Grandmother's sofa, Aunt Millie Dean's cherry table, the coat of arms on the kitchen wall by the never-used copper molds – the curved fish, the decorated ring, the gingerbread man that might have formed mousses or cakes but never had. Daddy had made that dark corner his, sitting grimly in the overstuffed armchair with his *Time* or his crosswords or staring out beyond the pale curtained window at the nothing at all that surrounded them. As a child, Barney's heart had moved toward that silent and frightened man with inarticulate love, unable to look him in the eyes.

Later, after his coronary, Daddy's place had become the painted brass bed in the corner bedroom, where he lay and smoked Viceroys in a holder and continued his grim solutions to crossword puzzles in magazines and almost never spoke. Mother had completely become his voice: 'Your father doesn't think much of the fall programs, Barney,' or 'Your father believes the economy is headed for a slump.' But he never heard Daddy say anything.

Barney led the ghosts out onto the terrace. Mother gave a polite gasp at the view of the Hotel Pierre, rising to the right of the General Motors building. Two pigeons flew up from the floor of the cedar decking. The terrace was splendid on this June morning; the ivy on its fence glistened in the bright sun; its scarlet geraniums glowed.

'You certainly have a lovely apartment, Barney,' Mother said. As usual her voice held back somehow in the praise. There was a 'Yes, but . . .' in it, if only by inflection.

For years he had ignored the way Mother gave with her words and took away with her voice. But now he said, 'What's wrong with it, Mother?'

Daddy was seating himself carefully in one of the lava gray deck chairs, as though, even dead, he had to protect himself from exertion.

Mother looked shocked, then reproachful. 'I didn't say there was anything *wrong*, Barney . . .'

Anger hit him suddenly and unexpectedly. 'Damn it, Mother!' he said, astonished at the strength in his voice. 'I *heard* the way you said it.'

She looked powerless but she came back instantly. 'I wish you wouldn't use that kind of language, Barney. I know that times have changed since we passed on, but your father . . .'

'Fuck my father,' Barney said. 'It's you I'm talking to, Mother.'

At the word 'fuck' his mother gasped and fluttered her hand over her heart. For a moment she became Blanche DuBois, raped by Stanley Kowalski.

Barney glanced toward Daddy and saw his face frozen in pain. 'I'm sorry, Mother,' he said. 'I shouldn't have said that.'

Mother's relief was immediate. She became Lady Bountiful at once. 'Oh, I suppose people talk that way all the time now,' she said, as if her absence from the living had produced the degeneration in standards she had always expected it would. 'It's just that we're not used to it is all.'

He was wondering how she could know how people talked nowadays when she said, 'Some things do come through to us, you know. Not a whole lot.'

'Where are you when you're not here?' he asked. 'Is it Purgatory?'

'Oh, no,' she said. 'It's not Purgatory. Your father and I don't even know if there *is* a Purgatory. We're in a quiet place,' she said, with the old hint of a whine in her voice, as if she were trying to tell him something too painful for words. That he didn't write to her often enough?

He had shown them the whole apartment now, in the ten minutes since he had prayed to see them and they had, surprisingly, stepped out of the elevator. He had had no idea such things were possible, yet accepted it easily enough. There had been a lot of new and surprising things in his life lately and this was another of them.

He had only lived in the apartment six weeks, here on the Upper East Side between Fifth and Madison, with skylights and high ceilings and marble fireplaces. A year before he had been living in an old house near a small Ohio town, wishing he were dead. Now he had an $1,800-a-month apartment, was a slim fifty-one years old, had grown a beard. The folk art paintings on his walls alone had cost more than his annual salary as a professor. The apartment was the top floor of what had once been a millionaire's mansion. Barney had made the money by writing a book about viruses that had, wildly, become a best seller for thirty-seven months. Two Nobel laureates had pronounced it the best work on the subject ever written.

'It certainly is nice to have a terrace,' Mother was saying. 'If only Gwen were here to enjoy it. Gwen always liked being outdoors.'

So that had been it. The 'but.' 'Gwen can go outdoors in Ohio any time she wants to, Mother,' he said. 'She has three acres all to herself.'

Mother looked hurt. 'You know what I mean, Barney.'

Immediately he felt the stab of guilt that Mother had clearly wanted him to feel. He buried it. 'Gwen is well rid of me,' he said. 'And I'm happy with Isabel.'

'It's too bad we can't meet Isabel. I suppose that when a woman goes out to a job . . .'

He could have brained her with a two-by-four. 'Can you stay for an hour?' he said.

That caught her by surprise and she turned to Daddy. 'I don't really know. What do you think, Allston?'

Daddy grunted some sort of assent, his first vocalization since arriving. Mother turned back to Barney and said, 'Well, I suppose it'll be all right. No more than an hour.'

'Good,' Barney said, with triumph. 'I'll call Isabel and tell her to jump in a cab. We can all have lunch together.'

'Barney!' Mother said. 'You're such a child. We don't need lunch. We're dead.'

Isabel arrived breathless but poised. In her tight Sasson jeans and T-shirt her figure was stunning; her face, without makeup, framed by curly gray hair that matched her gray eyes, was luminous. Gwen's waist was thick, her face solid and plain; she had a comforting look to her, domestic and tranquil. Isabel looked like a movie star on a day off. Gwen dyed her hair; Isabel glowed in gray.

'Mother and Daddy,' Barney said, 'I'd like you to meet Isabel.' Isabel looked at their faces wonderingly. She had seen photographs of them. 'Jesus!' she said. She held out a hand to Mother.

Mother was cool. 'I'm sorry, dear, but there's no touching.'

Isabel looked up to his face. 'What's going on, love?'

'It's real, honey,' he said. 'Hard to believe. But you get used to it.'

'I'd like a glass of wine,' Isabel said.

The four of them sat on the terrace. A blue jay perched itself on one corner of the fence, facing itself toward Central Park. The sky was a perfect blue. There was no breeze. Mother's hands were folded in her lap, over the pleats of the blue rayon dress. Daddy stared at the middle distance. Isabel sipped her wine, Barney his coffee. The black cat, Amagansett, came to the open French doors and crouched himself toward the jay, motionless.

'Is your accent British?' Mother said at last to Isabel. It was a fencing question; if Isabel's accent were *not* British de Gaulle had been Japanese.

Isabel nodded over her wine. 'Scottish.'

'Such a civilized country,' Mother said. 'With the lochs.' She pronounced it *lox*.

'Mmmm,' Isabel said and set her wineglass down on the deck.

'Yes,' Mother said, somehow satisfied by the exchange. She had managed to remove for herself any threats that Scotland might have for her and was ready to get down to business. 'Are the two of you married? I don't want to be rude.'

'No, Mother,' Barney said. 'We have no plans to be married.'

Mother pursed her lips. 'You're very . . . liberated,' she said.

'Oh, come on, Mother. It's no big deal and you know it.'

'*Barney*,' Mother said. 'I'm not thinking about what other people do. And God knows you're *old* enough to do as you like.'

He looked at her. She was Mother all right, with the dewlaps at her neck – or wattles, or whatever they were – and the pink-painted and wrinkled lips in a kind of pout. He had seen that pout a hundred times on the streets of New York. She sat now in the deck chair with her knees a foot apart and the hem of her rayon dress pulled back. He could see the sagging white flesh of her inner thighs above her rolled-down beige nylons. He turned his head away, pretending to look at the blue jay. 'Then what are you thinking of, Mother?' he said.

'Of your health, Barney,' she said, and he looked back at her own rampant unhealthiness. 'Of the doctors who told me you should take it easy, should not excite yourself . . .'

My God, he thought. *That again*. 'Mother,' he said aloud, 'I've had cardiograms yearly for thirty years. I don't have rheumatic heart anymore.' Yet in her presence he hardly believed it. 'I'm not a sick child.' But the words lacked conviction.

Isabel stood up and stretched. 'I've got to get back to work at the museum,' she said. Isabel was a director of the American Museum of Folk Art; Barney had been in love with her for nearly a year. She was forty-three, twice divorced, with a PhD in Art History from Glasgow and a perfect bottom. 'Good-bye, Mrs Witt and Mr Witt,' she said. 'Your son's a terrific lover.' She finished off her wine at a gulp and left. No one had eaten lunch.

'Well,' Mother said, 'she certainly is up-to-date. I see she feels comfortable without a bra.'

'Come off it, Mother,' he said. 'Are you trying to tell me she's a whore?'

Mother looked away with a grimace. 'Times change,

81

Barney,' she said, as though they didn't. 'I just hope you're sure she's what you really want.'

'I hear you, Mother,' he said. 'You said that about my first bicycle, the red one.'

'It's just that your father and I want you to make up your own mind about what's right for you . . .'

'My father hasn't said anything about Isabel,' he said. It was something new for him to speak like that and he felt a sense of exceeding proper limits. But he did not look at his father, the pathetic and silent figure in the chair.

'I know how your father feels about you,' she said. 'We've been married a long time.'

'How are your . . . your existences, now?' he said, changing the subject.

She brightened a bit. 'Your father rests well,' she said. 'I still seem to have my old difficulty sleeping.' As far as he could remember, his mother slept all right. She only liked complaining about not sleeping, about 'tossing and turning.' 'You know, Barney,' she went on, 'where we stay now sometimes our forms change and we become different ages of our lives. Sometimes I'm the age I was before you were born. And sometimes your father and I become babies, just little fat things with diapers on. When that happens I just sleep and sleep.'

'Wow!' he said, genuinely astonished. 'Do you have any control over it?'

'Well, yes. It's more or less a matter of willing it.'

'But, my God,' he said, 'then how can you have a sleeping problem? You can make yourself an infant whenever you want to and just sleep.' He shook his head in exasperation. 'Like a baby.'

She pursed her lips. 'It just doesn't seem *right*, Barney. For a grown-up person . . .' Her voice trailed off in a way he recognized, a way that meant, *Don't pry into my sorrows, Barney. I have sensitivities you wouldn't understand.*

When she was living he wouldn't have persisted, but things were different now. 'Come on, Mother,' he said. 'If you really wanted to sleep it certainly wouldn't strain your dignity to be a baby.' Then the stupidity, the narrowness of her struck him and he said, 'Jesus, there's something terrific about being a baby for a while.'

She shook her head adamantly, giving the look that meant, 'I knew you wouldn't understand.' Finally she said, in a confidential and pained voice, 'Barney. There's no one to change the diaper. It's . . . humiliating.'

He stared at her in disbelief. *Of course. All those matches in the bathroom, those bottles of Air Wick*. The way she made him run the lavatory tap when he peed, and aim for the edge of the toilet, so she couldn't hear it. The horror on her face if he farted.

And then something else struck him. 'You're both the same ages you were when you died. Why don't you make yourselves younger? Why be *old*?'

She looked at him wonderingly and for a moment her everlasting guard seemed to be down. 'Why not be old?' she said.

It rushed upon him, overwhelmed him. There they sat, on his New York terrace, both in their physical sixties, with pale, sagging bodies, false teeth, bags under their eyes. And by choice. They could be whatever age they wanted to be in whatever Limbo they had their existence.

He stared at her. 'Make yourself young for me, Mother,' he said.

She seemed not to hear him. She had fallen into some kind of guarded reverie.

Throughout his adult life Barney had suffered a frustrating disparity between sexual desire and sexual performance. Years before, a psychiatrist had uncovered memories of Barney's mother undressing in front of him, when Barney himself had been three and four years old and had slept in a cot in Mother's room. 'Now don't peek, Barney,' she would say, and pull her dress over her head. He always did peek, at the peach-colored slips, the flared rayon panties, the dark triangle of hair between her legs.

When, in the psychiatrist's office, he tried to remember his mother's face at those times, tried to remember more than her hips and breasts and underwear, he was never able to. He could not remember his mother with a face other than the sagging old woman's face her ghost now wore.

'What was that, Barney?' Mother said, smiling faintly.

'Could you make yourself young for me?' He tried to keep his voice casual, but he could hear the strain in it.

Mother looked at him sharply. Then she smiled. 'How young?'

He was flustered. 'I don't know. Young.'

'Well, it's sort of silly. But I'll try.' Her face made a little pout of concentration. She put her knees together, sat up straight in the chair, squinted her eyes shut.

For a moment her body and clothes, in the still sunlight of the terrace, became murky and dark, shrinking. And then before him sat, in a middy blouse and pleated cotton skirt, a little girl of about twelve. She had a blue ribbon in her hair and her face was bright, pretty, well-scrubbed, pink-cheeked. She wore black shoes with buckles and little white socks.

The blue jay flew away. The cat, startled, turned back toward the kitchen.

'Jesus!' Barney said, and turned toward Daddy. Daddy remained unchanged, not even looking at his child-wife.

'Well,' Mother said, 'how do you like me?'

He stared at her. She was a very pretty little girl, very proper, but with a flirtiness in her eyes. She had the same pout that she would wear as an old woman with false teeth and sagging jowls – a woman who never exercised, never walked except to shop for dresses in drab department stores. The flirtiness in her now was frank and not hidden. And the astonishing thing about her was the look of health.

'Jesus, Mother,' he said, 'I've never seen you look better.'

'Don't try to be funny, Barney,' she said. And then, astonishingly, she winked at him. 'Let me show you how I looked when I married your father.'

She shut her eyes again and her form melted and darkened and grew. And she sat in front of him then, his mother, as a beautiful flapper of twenty-five. She wore a cream-colored cloche hat over dark, shiny bangs and a low-cut, scoop-neck jersey dress with a short skirt, also cream-colored. Her hose were pale beige silk and her shoes silken. She had a long rope of white beads. Her face shone with health, with sex. She was the most beautiful woman he had ever seen in his life.

He stared at her. She was clearly his mother, yet so different. So beautiful – more beautiful than Isabel – with her long white throat, her high breasts.

She leaned forward toward him, confidentially. 'Barney,' she said, in a youthful, trilling voice – a theatrical, coquettish voice, 'I think I'd like a cigarette.'

'Sure,' he said weakly, and fumbled in his shirt pocket for a pack of Trues. He held the pack out to her and she reached out with scarlet fingernails and took one delicately. 'These dumb filter tips,' she said. 'I always smoked Sobranies, or Cubebs.' She laughed – a trilling, light, airy laugh.

Daddy was staring toward Central Park, his liver-spotted hands folded in his lap, his face set. Below his pants cuffs his clocked maroon socks were wrinkled over bony ankles.

Barney lit her True with his Cricket, then lit one himself. When she bent toward him he could see the edge of fine lace at the top of the beige chemise beneath her neckline and below that the hint of cleavage. He was becoming aroused. It did not frighten him. Somehow his spirit had moved imperceptibly to a place of no rules, here on this cedar deck in Manhattan with the spring sun heating the back of his neck.

Mother exhaled smoke open-mouthed; smoke curled in the sunlight around her face. She blinked her long lashes slowly, 'I think I'd like a drink, Barney,' she said. 'Let's go in the kitchen.'

Sometimes, as a child, he had heard that tone of voice; it had thrilled him then as it thrilled him now. It was a voice she could use on a picnic or when suddenly deciding that they should all forget about dinner at home and go to a movie and just eat candy and popcorn. Sometimes she would just drop the whole middle-class pretense, the whole anxious, fretful Motherhood role, and become for a while a lively, bouncy, sly person. And seeing it now, there with an erection pressing in his jeans, he knew that was the thing he had searched for in women, for years: the voice that said, 'What the hell, Barney, anything goes.'

He looked nervously for a moment toward his father, opened his mouth to speak.

And Mother said, 'Why don't you just stay here and rest for a while, Allston? It'll do you good.'

His father did not turn to face them. 'Whatever you want, Anna,' he said.

'Well then,' she said and stood, smoothing her dress along her behind, checking her stocking seams. 'Do you have any gin, Barney?' she said. 'I'd like a Gibson.'

'Sure,' he said. Leaving the terrace, he reached for her arm, to help her across the threshold, to touch her.

She pulled away. 'No touching, Barney,' she said. 'You mustn't touch the dead.'

The reminder was a shock, knotting his stomach. The whole Oedipus fantasy dissolved: getting his young mother drunk, running his hand up under her dress, along those pale silk stockings, lolling his tongue gently into her crimson mouth . . .

As he closed the French doors to the terrace she said, 'Your father was always a good man, Barney. But there were some things he never wanted to understand.'

He looked through the glass at Daddy, sadly. There the man sat, alone as ever.

He fixed her a big, dry Gibson with trembling hands, and another for himself. She leaned against the refrigerator, cupped the drink in both hands, giggled. Then she drank greedily and he fixed her another.

'My father was rich, you know,' she said.

'I know.' Her father had been a banker in Cleveland. There had been pictures of him everywhere at home. He had died before Mother married, had left his money to a young mistress.

'This dress was made by Coco Chanel. Daddy would take me to New York in the summers, and we'd stay right here at the Pierre.'

He was astonished at that. He did not remember her talking about New York. But he had never imagined his mother, his anxious, cheaply dressed mother, as this gorgeous flapper.

Abruptly she took off her hat with one hand and set it on the dishwasher. Then she shook her head and the shiny black hair, short, beautifully cut, framed her face. His penis began to harden again, but hopelessly. She was dead, untouchable, now that the word 'incest' was as meaningless to him, a virologist, as an obscure tribal taboo.

'It's warm in here,' she said, smiling. 'Fix me another drink and I'll take my clothes off for you.'

His hands shook so much that he spilled gin in the sink, on the floor. But he mixed the drink somehow, not looking at her. He could hear the sound of silken clothes, of stockinged legs rubbing together. He looked up at the Kliban Cat Calendar over the stainless steel sink: 'June, 1980' it read. In the morning he would have an appointment with his dentist. Isabel would be home from the museum in three hours. His penis ached. His whole body trembled.

When he turned, holding the drink out to her, he almost dropped it. She was still leaning back against the refrigerator but now her dress lay on the floor. She was wearing a beige silk chemise over her breasts – the breasts that had nursed him – and a matching silk half-slip, so short that the place where her garters stretched her stockings above her thighs was visible. She had kicked off her shoes and her legs and feet were beautiful.

She looped her thumbs under the waist of the slip as he stood there holding out the Gibson. Then she paused. 'Set the drink on the counter, Barney,' she said. She looked him over thoughtfully. 'You know, Barney,' she said. 'My father was a tall man like you. And rich, like you are now.'

'I know,' he said, in almost a whisper.

'He always bought my clothes for me. Never Mother. Always Daddy.'

'And you bought mine,' he said.

She smiled. 'That's right.'

'Take your slip off, Mother,' he said.

'Do you know, Barney?' she said. 'You're old enough, right now, to be my father.'

He thought about that a moment, here in this nice kitchen with its European fittings, its gray slate floor, its flawless white dishes. His trembling subsided, but not his penis. He began to take off his belt, unbuttoned the top button of his jeans. 'Well, Mother,' he said, as something in his chest seemed to open to the bright light in the kitchen, into the splendid vision of Eros in front of his gaze, 'love always finds a way.'

'Oh, yes,' she said, her voice trembling, bending her young body to pull down her slip with slim fingers. 'Oh, yes.'

Daddy

Barney came back out on the terrace. After their half hour together, Mother was asleep on the living room couch, regressed to an infant.

'Daddy,' Barney said. 'Why didn't you come and see me in the hospital?'

Daddy shifted his weight uneasily in the deck chair. 'Which hospital?' he said gruffly, not looking toward his son. He had never, when alive, looked toward his son while speaking to him.

'Oh, come on, Daddy,' Barney said. There was bravado in this familiarity; Daddy's edge was not easily overcome.

Daddy said nothing. He was looking in the direction of Central Park.

'It was the Children's Hospital, Daddy. Where they gave me the heat treatment for rheumatic fever. Where they almost killed me.'

'I remember,' Daddy said.

'Well, why didn't you come and see me?' Barney said. 'Why didn't you send me a postcard in that fine handwriting of yours? Or call me on the 'phone?'

There was silence for a while. Daddy's figure, for a moment, seemed to shimmer as Mother's had done when she had begun to change her form. But Daddy did not change. 'Nothing to say,' he said, finally.

Barney stared at him. To his surprise, he found himself crying. 'Anything,' he said. 'You could have said *anything*.'

Daddy shimmered again. 'Silly,' he said. 'Childish.'

'Daddy!' Barney cried. '*I needed you.*'

Daddy shimmered more seriously. Then he turned and looked at Barney. He was younger than before, slightly less gray. 'You were a Mama's boy,' he said. 'There was nothing for me to say to you.'

It took an effort for Barney to speak. 'You could have said "Hi." You could have mailed me a card that said "Get Well Soon."' Saying this, he felt a pain in his stomach, like a stitch. It grew and became a hot wire beneath his diaphragm. He began to sob, silently. He had been standing at the French doors; now, he seated himself in one of the director's chairs, arms around his middle, and squinted his eyes shut until the sobbing ended.

'You always were a crybaby, too,' Daddy said, as if stating the weather report.

Barney opened his eyes but could not speak. He stared at his father, who was younger now – definitely younger. Daddy was no longer wearing his serge suit. He wore a white sport shirt with an open collar and white flannel pants. He looked like Don Budge, ready for a set. His hair had lost almost all its gray. His socks were white; his shoes, black and white.

It was early afternoon and hot; there was sweat at the back of Barney's neck. He was wearing Levi's; they were too heavy for this June afternoon. He began taking his shoes off to cool his feet. 'I had a lot to cry about,' he said.

Daddy looked at him a moment. 'Who doesn't?' There was contempt in his voice. His eyes were pale blue. His face had lost twenty years while they were talking but the expression on the face had not changed: Daddy was angry, as he had always been. 'My father beat me with his walking stick and I didn't cry.'

'I'm sorry, Daddy,' Barney said. 'I'm sorry the son of a bitch beat you.' He sighed. There had been no relief in saying it. Maybe he wasn't sorry at all.

'I never finished high school,' Daddy was saying, looking toward Central Park again. There was a hint of suntan on his normally pale face, and the flesh of his jaw was tight, strong-looking. His hair was black and slick. 'My first job was unloading sacks of Portland cement for eighty cents a day. I saved money and bought the Encyclopedia Americana so I could know where the Suez Canal was and what the names of the chemical elements were. I lived on cheap food and slept on the floor. After

90

five years I bought my first car, a black Model A, and I was cheated on it; the differential was bent and when I drove it fast the axle broke and broke my left leg with it. When I married Anna – your mother – in nineteen twenty-four, I still walked with a limp and was still paying for that goddamned wrecked Ford.' He grimaced. 'I never even told anybody this before.'

'I'm glad you're telling me,' Barney said.

His father abruptly turned a hard, cruel face to him and looked directly at his eyes. 'Are you?' he said. 'Are you glad?'

Barney stared back at him, abashed. 'I don't know.'

'Good,' Daddy said, with relief. 'You can drop that psychotherapy horseshit. What you always wanted was to have Anna to yourself. Put your goddamned face against her tits.'

Barney set his shoes on the deck, then took a cigarette out of his pocket. He had never, in his lifetime, heard his father say words like 'tits.' Daddy had never once discussed sex with him – not in any way at all. From the time he was five his father had hardly spoken to him. He lit a cigarette. This conversation was overdue. The pain in his stomach had changed to rawness. His hands had stopped shaking. 'Daddy,' he said levelly, 'you didn't know how to keep her. I wanted her for myself.'

'What do you mean I didn't know how?' Daddy said. 'She never loved anybody.'

'Maybe her father,' Barney said.

Daddy looked at him a minute. 'Maybe you aren't so stupid after all.'

'I don't think she really wanted me either. I think she just liked teasing me. She never could let anything alone.'

Daddy was more relaxed now. 'I'll take one of your smokes,' he said.

'Sure,' Barney offered him the pack. There was an ease now in his stomach.

When Daddy lit up his whole body seemed to relax. It was wonderful to see – something Barney had waited to see for a long, long time.

'That goddamned woman could not make a sandwich without turning it into soap opera. She could not stop chattering and pissing and moaning. We would make love on Sunday mornings when you were at church with those crazy evangelists and she would have to get out of bed and put in her suppositories. Then when I got hard she had to get up and pull down the shades or take the phone off the hook. She said I was too animal for her spirit. I would tell her I loved her soul. It was all bullshit. Just bullshit.'

'Were you scared?' Barney was watching him. He began to shimmer again. Now he looked to be twenty years old, was wearing a white sweater and navy blue pants.

'I never knew what I felt when we were in bed,' Daddy said. 'She kept everything so goddamned *confused . . .*'

'I know.'

'*The hell you know.*' Daddy stood up, springy on his young legs, looked around the terrace. 'Get me a glass of gin.'

'You stopped drinking when I was eleven. You wouldn't even eat Aunt Sallie's fruitcake, because of the little shot of whiskey she used.'

'And I didn't cry about it, either. Get me that gin. It won't hurt now. I'm dead. God damn it to hell, I'm *dead*.'

When Barney gave him the gin, he asked, 'Are you in Limbo?'

Daddy took a long swallow before answering. His throat trembled with the gin going down. 'I suppose it is Limbo. There's nobody to tell you anything. You're free to come and go and to change around, but it doesn't mean anything anymore. Nothing means anything at all. It just goes on.'

'That's how you *lived*,' Barney said.

'Yes,' Daddy said. 'Maybe it's Hell. I don't know and don't care.'

Barney sat down and cried a moment. The tears came simply and easily; he mourned for his father's lost life and for his own, unable now to tell them apart. 'You blew it, Daddy,' he said. 'Why did you have to blow it? Why didn't you shut her up? Why didn't you hit her in the face?'

'I wasn't a brute,' Daddy said. 'And she was too much for me.' He finished off the glass and handed it back. 'Barney,' he said, 'to tell the truth, *you* were too much for me. I'm no father. Nobody taught me to be a father. They talked about responsibility and I didn't know anything about a noisy kid with a diaper full of shit. They told me about the love of a man for a woman but I didn't know what to do with that neurotic bitch. *She talked all the time.* It was like she walked around rubbing herself. Twitching. And she aroused me so much. At the movies she would put her hand in my pocket and squeeze me and then we'd go home and she wouldn't let me touch her.'

There were tears coming down his father's cheeks and his face was bright red. He seemed only fifteen years old now, and was wearing a frayed white shirt with no collar, and knickers. 'I would go to the bathroom and . . . abuse myself.'

Barney had never talked to anyone in his life this way. He was covered with goosebumps. 'I jacked off in that bathroom, too,' he said, with the words coming easily, relievingly. 'Afterward I'd look in the bathroom mirror and I would hate myself. I was disgusted. I thought if you ever found out you would never speak to me again.'

His father's voice was very youthful now. It was the voice of a boy at puberty, cracking into high pitch from time to time. 'I could never get that part of myself *clean* enough.' For a moment he looked as though he were going to vomit. He was about ten years old now, and smaller. 'And I never wanted any of that . . . disturbance.'

'I know,' Barney said. 'I know how that feels.'

Daddy held out his short arms and looked at them. He was wearing a middy blouse and short pants. There was no hair on his arms and the hair on his head was neatly combed, jet black. Then he looked toward Barney shyly. 'This is the way I like to be. This way or old. I don't want the things in between.'

Daddy stood there in front of him as a child, scrubbed and slightly pretty. He looked up at Barney, shook his head. 'I don't want to be a baby. Not yet.'

He shimmered and then began to darken, to melt and flow in the bright afternoon light. After a moment he was an old man again in blue serge and with liver-spotted wrists. His face was deeply lined, weak, both hurt and angry. He seated himself cautiously. 'Get me another drink. But mix it with something this time.'

Barney got him gin and orange juice and stirred it with one of the silver spoons he had inherited from Mother. He went into the living room to check her out. She was still a three-month-old infant, chubby and scowling, with a wet thumb in her mouth and her body on its side in the fetal position. Both her small fists were clenched.

She slept on the black Chesterfield couch; he had pushed two dining chairs against it to keep her from falling off. Above her the huge living room windows looked out on two mansions with dark mansard roofs – older, most likely, than she. He reached down and felt her diaper; it was still dry.

On the terrace Daddy said, 'My father was a state senator; he was an old man when I was born. My mother was his third wife and was far beneath him socially. She took in wash when she was a girl.'

'I know.' Barney had heard this before, but never from Daddy.

Daddy flashed a look at him – the same silent look he had always given Barney as a child. 'What in hell do *you* know?' he said.

Barney sighed; his father had never *said* that before, had only burdened him with the silent weight of his contempt. 'Right now,' Barney said levelly, 'I know more than you ever did know. More than you ever will. Your life was sheltered, and you hardly lived it.'

His father's face darkened even more and he clenched a fist. 'Don't threaten me,' Barney said. 'I can take her away from you.'

Daddy turned his head away, forced a grim laugh. 'Take her,' he said. 'You're what she wanted anyway. A mama's boy with poetry in his soul. An oversexed

94

crybaby.'

Barney looked at his set face, his lined face, and saw clearly the weakness in it. 'You self-serving son of a bitch,' he said.

'You're a weak sister and you know it, Barney,' his father said. 'You never had the guts to make your own way.'

. 'You used to wet the *bed* when you took us on trips in the car. You'd get drunk on wine in tourist courts and sleep with your clothes on and wet your *pants*. You acted tough with me when I was eight but you cringed with every mailman or shoe clerk when you were in the real world . . .'

Daddy lurched forward and shouted, '*You* cringed when I came home from work and caught you sitting in the kitchen with her. You'd be drying the silver or telling her about yourself – and she'd be smiling at you like a goddamned vamp. And you'd see me come in and you'd fidget because I caught you in your goddamned gigolo act.' He paused, and then said, 'You can *have* her.'

Barney stared at him. 'You don't mean that. You can't live in Limbo alone. And you never had anybody else but her. You could have had me . . .' His throat constricted without warning, and his eyes began to burn. '. . . But you didn't want me. You put me in that hospital and hoped you'd never see me again.'

Daddy seemed now to be somehow subdued – nearly at peace. He said nothing to Barney's accusation. He finished his drink. When he handed him the empty glass there was a note of resignation in the gesture, but he said nothing.

Barney took the glass and stood up. 'Do you want another?'

His father nodded. 'The same.'

'Daddy,' Barney said. 'I love you. I loved you more than I ever loved her . . .'

His father nodded silently.

Mother was awake now, her eyes staring upward,

unfocused. She lay on her back, grasping; her small hands greedily opened and shut. He did not speak to her. She remained silent, wrapped up in her own thoughts, or plans . . .

He fixed gin and orange juice and made himself a cup of instant coffee. The pain was in his stomach. He had always loved that man out there. He had loved him when they flew kites together at the Embarcadero, had loved him when the man took him to see Eddie Cantor at the Fox Theatre on Market Street. He had ridden on Daddy's back in the living room, rejoicing at Daddy's warmth, Daddy's strength. And then, about the time of kindergarten, Daddy had started drinking every night. Once Barney had tried to climb on his back and Daddy had shoved him across the room. Barney had sat down and bawled and his father, huge and now terrifying, had thundered over to him and slapped his face twice and said, 'Cry for your Mama; don't cry in front of me. Or I'll give you something to cry about.' His breath stank. The rage in his voice was an earthquake.

Standing in the kitchen under the skylight, now, facing the Cat Calendar with 1980 written on it, Barney began crying again. He set the gin and orange juice down on the dishwasher and wept.

And then he heard a sound like the sound of his own crying and turned around, facing the pass-through into the living room. Mother, his greedy infant mother, her face red and twisted, was crying with him. She cried a baby's cry, furious at a world that did not continuously serve her wishes.

When he came out onto the terrace again it was a half hour later. He had decided to make himself a drink, and then another. His mother stopped crying, fell asleep again; her compact, narcissistic self was turned away from him, toward the black back of the couch. He carried two glasses with him: both were rich in gin.

The terrace was very hot. It was midafternoon and the

sun was ferocious. Daddy had taken off his coat and sat in rolled-up white shirt-sleeves, still wearing his dark blue tie.

Barney did not feel drunk so much as he felt ready for anything. Anything at all. 'Here's your drink.' He held the glass out and Daddy took it with a curt nod. He seated himself and stared for a while at the green roof of the Hotel Pierre above the terrace fence. Isabel's black cat came through the French doors and began to explore some ivy leaves near the deck; he would look up hopefully from time to time as birds flew overhead and then would seem sad that none flew down to him. He must feel, Barney thought, that the world owes him a bird now and then. And maybe it does, since the world made him a cat.

'Daddy,' he said, 'I want to tell you about the pyrotherapy they gave me when I was ten.'

'Why bring that up now?' his father said wearily.

'Because you wouldn't let me tell you before. When you picked me up at the train station.'

'You were chattering away like your mother. And I had to drive. It was rush hour.'

'It always was.'

'What good would it do to tell me?'

'I'll decide that.'

His father scowled, began to shimmer. Quickly Barney got up, reached out, took the glass from Daddy's iridescent hand. 'I'll pour your drink out if you don't stop that.'

The shimmering stopped. Barney gave him back the drink.

'You need me to want you here in the world, don't you? Or back you go to Limbo where there aren't any drinks.'

Daddy scowled and did not answer.

'They put me into a kind of homemade machine of brown-painted steel. It was half a cylinder and it covered my body from neck to ankles. I was flat on a hospital bed. They had already wrapped me tightly in a gray wool Army blanket and I was stifling with the heat of that before they even threw the switch on.

97

'There were about forty light bulbs screwed into sockets under the curved top of that brown thing, Daddy, and when they turned them on and the heat came pouring into that blanket it was unbearable. My hands were strapped to my sides under the blanket, so I wouldn't hurt myself when I had convulsions, or break the light bulbs . . .' He realized that he was sweating profusely. He set his drink on the deck and took off his shirt, wiped his wet chest with it, dabbed at his neck.

'Daddy,' he said, 'I've been afraid of heat all my adult life. They kept me in that thing fourteen hours a day for two weeks. Each day they brought my internal temperature up to a hundred seven. There was no clock in the room and when I'd ask the attendant what time it was she'd be cross with me. So I lay there and tried to count off the time in my head, a second at a time. Each minute was longer than I could imagine. I prayed to die, tried to will myself dead.'

Daddy shifted his weight in the chair, sipped his drink. He rolled up his sleeves another notch, showing pale bony arms, with fine gray hairs on them and brown spots, like big freckles. The cat sniffed at an ivy leaf.

'The doctor had supervised my first day in the machine: the treatment was a project of hers – later abandoned, as too dangerous. She was like a Nazi, Daddy – a Nazi doctor who had me given to her. She said you had signed the authorization for the treatment.' He looked at his father, sweat pouring down his forehead into his eyes. The afternoon sun was murderous.

His father did not look at him. He raised his drink slowly to his old, pale lips. Then Barney, moving very quickly, reached out and, with the edge of his right hand knocked the drink from his father's weak grip. The glass flew across the terrace and smashed into the side of the fence. The cat spun around and fled into the house.

'The doctor said you'd come and see me on the weekend, Daddy. For the first five days I held in my mind a picture of you holding a glass of water for me while I lay under that torture box. But you didn't come.'

His father turned, shocked by the lost drink, and looked at him open-mouthed. He looked hopelessly old, frail, vulnerable. 'You worthless bastard,' Barney said. 'You didn't come. I want you to rot in hell for it.'

'I was sick,' his father said.

'You were not sick, Daddy. You were drunk. You were sitting in your moss-green overstuffed chair in the living room on that Saturday, drinking gin. That was June 17, 1938. It was the worst day I've ever lived, and it soiled my life.'

'You're making a soap opera out of it, like your mother. Doctor Morton did charity work with poor children. She was no Nazi. You've built it up in your mind.'

'That's horseshit, Daddy. The next kid they tried it on died, the poor bastard. After five days of it. I told you that in the car, in Dayton, when I got there on the train after the year in the hospital.'

'I don't remember . . .'

'You remember moving out of the goddamned *state* after you and that flirt in there put me in the hospital, don't you? And you never . . .' Barney leaned forward, saying each word carefully. '. . . And you never wrote me a single word. When I tried to tell you about how I had gone through that treatment and *hadn't cried once*, the way you would have wanted me to, you told me to be quiet because you had to drive the fucking *car*. Daddy,' he said, '*I didn't cry*.'

'Those were tough times. It was the Depression . . .'

'The Jews in Auschwitz treated their children with more concern, Daddy. Most of them did.' He turned his face away from his father's and looked toward the Pierre. 'Some of them might have been looking, like you were, for somebody to blame.'

'Blame for what?' Daddy's voice sounded weaker.

'For the way your life fell apart. For marrying that Goddamned woman in there. For the way she stole your balls from you right in front of your eyes. So you could call me a Mama's boy . . .'

99

'You *were* a Mama's boy. Still are.' There was a tremor now in the voice. 'I know what the two of you were doing an hour ago in the kitchen.'

Barney turned toward him. 'That's right, Daddy. We climaxed together. It was wonderful.'

'Bullshit,' Daddy said. His voice shook. His face was gray.

Barney suddenly began to laugh. 'Maybe you can't believe it.'

'She was frigid. It was the way she was brought up . . .'

'Bullshit,' Barney said, laughing. 'She wasn't frigid for *me*, you cowardly son of a bitch.'

Suddenly his father's face twisted in pain and his pale hand went to his chest, squeezing at the shirt pocket. His lips were blue.

Barney stared at him. 'You can't have a heart attack when you're dead,' he said.

Daddy choked and fell off the chair onto the deck. He lay there, silently writhing, for several minutes. His hands were white; they clenched into fists and unclenched rhythmically. After a while a kind of foam began to appear on Daddy's lips; his face was ghastly. His eyes stared upward toward the sky. He made no sound. Then, abruptly, he twitched over on one side, toward where Barney sat. Barney stared at him. His age had not changed but his position was now fetal. Barney remembered a time forty years before when as a small child he had seen his father lying like that in the bed of a cheap California motor court; his body had been pressed into a wet stain on the rumpled sheet. Barney remembered the smell.

'*Oh, my God, Daddy,*' he said aloud, looking down at his father, '*you're just like she is. You're a goddamned infant. You always were.*'

A blue jay was chattering somewhere beyond the terrace fence. The black cat came softly back outside into the sun and walked toward Daddy. There came a soft, hissing sound from Daddy's throat and then a hoarse, convulsive shuddering, and then silence. The cat nudged

Daddy with his nose and then began to purr. Daddy was clearly dead.

Barney heard footsteps from the French doors and turned to look. Mother was there, as a middle-aged woman in a cheap dress. She spoke through loose false teeth. 'It looks as if Allston's died again,' she said, matter-of-factly.

'How can that be . . . ?' Barney said.

Mother shook her head worriedly. 'I don't know, Barney, but it happens to both of us all the time where we are. The same deaths.'

Barney stared at her. 'Then you have to go through lung cancer?'

Mother pursed her lips. 'Often,' she said.

'Jesus!' Barney said. 'Then maybe it isn't Limbo at all. Maybe it's Hell.'

'Best not to know,' Mother said, briskly. 'I've got to get him back now, and get back myself. Strict rules.' She looked away from him toward the Hotel Pierre and began to shimmer. 'My Daddy always stayed at the Pierre,' she said, wistfully. 'And there were always flowers in his room.' As her body began to fade, Barney glanced down and saw that Daddy's dead body was fading too. There was shattered glass on the deck. He felt tears again, just beginning.

He looked back to Mother, who was now translucent. 'I loved him, Mother,' he said. 'I still love him.'

She smiled at him flirtatiously. 'What we did in the kitchen was naughty,' she said. She winked at him.

'*Damn you*,' he said. 'It's him I love. It's *Daddy*.'

She was hardly visible now, and her voice was faint, far away. 'It's not for you to have him, Barney,' she said. 'Daddy's *mine*.' And they were both gone.

After twenty minutes, Barney stopped crying. Something had ended for him. He stayed in his chair for the rest of the afternoon, tremulously, testing his new life. Toward suppertime, when Isabel would be coming home from work, he began to whistle.

From time to time he looked up at the Hotel Pierre, which rose with great clarity into the New York sky.

The Apotheosis of Myra

Out beyond the French windows during the day's second
sunset the grass began singing. It had begun as a hum and
as it gained in strength quickly became song. Edward
pushed the French windows farther open and stepped out
onto the terrace. Lovely there now, with a sky dark blue
like an Earth sky. And, frightening though it was, the
singing too was lovely – melodic, slow-tempoed, a sort of
insistent lullaby. In three years here he had heard about it;
this was the first time he had ever heard it. He sipped from
the glass of gin in his hand. He was half drunk and that
made it easier to take than it might have been. An
enormous plain of dark grass lay before him in twilight,
motionless, singing. No one knew the language. But it was
clearly a language.

After a few minutes Myra came out from the living
room, moving stiffly and rubbing her eyes. She had been
asleep on the couch. 'Goodness!' she said. 'Is that the
grass?'

'What else?' he said, turning away from her. He finished
his drink.

Myra's voice was excited. 'You know, Edward, I heard
a recording of this . . . this grass. Back in college, years
ago. It was before anybody had even heard of Endolin.'
She was trying to make her voice sound lively, but she
could not override the self-pity in it. Myra, Edward felt,
swam in self-pity as a goldfish swam in water. It was her
own transparent medium. 'It was in a course called "The
Exploration of our Galaxy," I think. Dull as dishwater.
But the professor played some records of life forms, and I
still remember Belsin grass.' Belsin was the name of the
planet. 'There was a question about it on the midterm.
What are you drinking there, Edward?'

He did not look at her. 'Gin and tonic. I'll get you one.'

He walked along the moonwood deck past her and into the house. The liquor was in the kitchen. During the last year he had taken to bringing a case at a time out of the storage room, where supplies from Earth were kept. There was the half-empty last case of Gordon's gin and a nearly empty one of Johnnie Walker side by side on the kitchen counter next to a stack of unwashed dishes. The dishwasher had broken down again and he hadn't felt like trying to fix it. He grinned wryly, looking at the pile of dirty Haviland that Myra had insisted on bringing with her out to this godforsaken part of the galaxy. If he could get her to do the dishwashing he might not kill her. Fat chance.

The idea of killing her was fairly recent. Originally he had thought the arthritis and the self-pity and the booze would do it for him. But Belsin had worked for her far better than he had expected, with the fresh Endolin that had made her demand to come in the first place. Endolin was a scraggly little plant and the finest pain-killer and anti-inflammation drug ever known. It grew only on Belsin and did not travel well even in total vacuum. Myra was rich and her family was powerful; she had provided the money and her grandfather the power to get him the job here. She was thirty-four and had had violently painful arthritis since the age of six.

He made her drink, as usual, stronger than his own. There was no ice, since that wasn't working either.

She had seated herself on the moonwood bench when he got back out on the terrace and was looking at the stars, her head slightly inclined toward the singing of the grass. For a moment he paused; she was really very beautiful. And the look of self-pity had gone from her face. He had loved her, once, when she was like this. He hadn't married her only for her money. The singing had become softer. It would end soon, if what he had heard about it was true. It happened so rarely, though, that everything about it was uncertain and no one had the foggiest notion of how the grass did it in the first place, let alone why.

Myra smiled at him, not even reaching for the drink. 'It sings so . . . *intelligently*,' she said, smiling. 'And feelingfully.' She took the drink finally and set it on the moonwood bench beside her. Moonwood was not really wood; it was sliced from quarries and outcroppings near Belsin's north pole. You could drive nails into it and even build houses from it. Their house, though, was a prefab, cut from steel and glass in a factory in Cleveland and shipped out here, for a king's ransom.

'And nobody knows why it sings?' she said.

'Correct,' Edward said. 'How are your hands?'

She smiled dreamily toward him. 'Very good.' She flexed them. 'Hardly any pain at all. And my neck is easy tonight. Supple.'

'Congratulations,' he said, without feeling. He walked over to one of the deck chairs and seated himself. The problem with killing her was not the killing itself. That would be very easy out here, on a planet with only a few hundred settlers. The problem was in making it totally unambiguous, clear and simple and with himself blameless, so he could inherit. The laws concerning extraterrestrial death were a mess. One little snag could keep it in court for thirty years.

'You know what I'd like to do, Edward?' she said.

He took a swallow from his drink. 'What's that?'

'I'd like to get out the EnJay and take a ride to the orchids.'

'Christ!' he said. 'Isn't it pretty late?' She had not ridden in the EnJay for a year or more. 'And doesn't the bouncing hurt your legs? And back?'

'Edward,' she said, 'I'm better. Really.'

'Okay,' he said. 'I'll get a bottle. And some Endolin.'

'Forget the Endolin for now,' she said brightly. 'I'll be all right.'

The Nuclear Jeep was in a moonwood shed at the back of the house, next to the dark-green Mercedes and the two never-used bicycles. He backed the jeep out, shifted gears, and scratched off around the house. In the low gravity of Belsin scratching off was difficult to do but he had learned the trick. He pulled up to the turnaround in front of the house where Myra's elevator normally let her out and was astonished to see her walking down the stairs, one hand on the banister, smiling toward him.

'Well!' he said as she got into the jeep.

'Pretty good, huh?' she said, smiling. She squeezed his arm.

He drove off with a jerk and across the obsidian surface of their front yard. Much of Belsin was obsidian; it was in fissures in that glasslike surface that the Endolin grew. At the end of the yard a winding path, barely wide enough for the jeep, went through the Belsin grass, which was still singing, but much more softly. He liked driving the path, with its glassy low traction and its narrow and often wrongly banked curves. There was hardly any way to build a real road on Belsin. You could not cut Belsin grass – which wasn't grass at all and seemed to grow out of the granitic rock beneath it like hair – and if you drove on it it screamed and bled. Bringing from Earth the equipment to grade and level the obsidian would have been almost enough to bankrupt even Myra's family. So when you drove on Belsin you used a car with a narrow axle, and you followed the natural vein-like pathways on the planet's surface. There weren't many places to drive *to* anyway.

The singing, now that they were driving with the grass on either side of them, was remarkable. It was like a great chorus of small voices, or a choir chanting at the edge of understanding, alto and soprano. It was vaguely spiritual, vaguely erotic, and the truly remarkable thing about it was that it touched the human feelings so genuinely. As with Endolin, which magically dovetailed so well with the products of terrestrial evolution, producing a molecule that fit a multichambered niche in the human nervous system as if made for it, the grass seemed to have been ready for humanity when humanity first landed on Belsin sixty years before. Captain Belsin himself had heard it during the first explorations. The grass had sung for that old marauding tycoon and he had written in his journal

106

the now famous words, 'This planet speaks my language.' When Endolin had been found, years later, it had seemed fitting that the planet, able somehow to touch human feeling with its astonishing music, could also provide one of the great anodynes. Endolin was hard to come by, even in the richest obsidian fields, but it was nearly perfect when fresh. It could all but obliterate physical pain without affecting the reason or the perceptions. And there was no hangover from it. Myra's life on Earth had been hell. Here, it was passable.

'Boy, do I feel good!' Myra said. 'I think I could dance till dawn.'

He kept his eyes on the road, following it with the wheel. 'In an hour you'd be screaming from the pain. You're forgetting how Endolin burns out.' That was its great drawback, and he was glad to remind her of it. That, and the fact that you couldn't take it constantly. If you did it paralyzed you.

For a moment she sounded crushed. 'Honey,' she said, 'I haven't forgotten.' Then she brightened. 'But lately my bad hours between pills have been easier.'

'That's good,' he said. He tried to put conviction in it.

After a while they were driving along a ridge from which they could see, far off to the right, the lights of the Endolin packing plant and the little spaceport beside it.

'I didn't know they worked at *night*,' Myra said.

'For the last six months they have.'

'Six months Earth time?' There was Belsin time, with its seventeen-hour day and short year, and there was Earth time. Edward had a way of shifting from one to the other without warning.

'Earth time,' he said, as if talking to a child.

'You almost never tell me about your work, Edward,' she said. 'Have orders gone up?'

'Yes,' he said. 'Business is booming. We're sending out a shipload every month now.' He hesitated and then said, 'Earth time.'

'That's terrific, Edward. It must make you feel . . . useful to be so successful.'

He said nothing. It made no difference to him how well the business did, except that more shippings meant more supplies of gin and of television tapes and things like peanut butter and coffee and caviar from Earth. Nothing on Belsin could be eaten. And the only business – the only real reason for humanity to be there at all – was Endolin.

'Will you have to increase the number of workers?' Myra said. 'To keep up with bigger harvests?'

He shook his head. 'No. The equipment has been improved. Each man brings in two or three pounds a day now. Faster vehicles and better detectors.'

'That's *fascinating*!' Myra said, sitting upright with a slight wince of pain. 'I had no idea what was going on.'

'You never asked,' he said.

'No,' she said, 'I suppose I didn't.'

They drove on northward in silence for a long time listening to the grass. Edward himself, despite his hidden anger and his frustrations, became calmed by it. Finally Myra spoke. 'Listening to that singing is . . . is amazing,' she said softly. 'It seems to go very deep. You know' – she turned abruptly in her seat to face him – 'the more I take Endolin the more . . . mystical my feelings are. Or spiritual.' She looked a little self-conscious saying it probably because she knew how impatient he was with her interests in poetry and in music. And in reincarnation.

'It's bound to affect your mind . . .' he said.

'No,' she said. 'I know that's not it. It's something I've had since I was a child. Sometimes after the arthritic pain I'd have a . . . a burned-out feeling in my nerves and a certain clarity in my head. I would lie in my bed in the hospital or whatever and I felt I knew things just the other side of the edge of knowing.'

He started to speak and glanced over at her. He saw that she had not finished the drink she was carrying. That was unusual, since Myra was close to being an alcoholic – something he encouraged in her. He decided to say nothing.

'I lost those feelings when I got older,' she went on. 'But lately I've been getting them back. Stronger. And th grass, singing like that, seems to encourage it.' She stopped for a minute. 'You know,' she said, 'the grass is giving me the same feeling. That something on the other side of knowledge can really be known. If we could only . . . only relax somehow and clear our minds and grasp it.'

Edward's voice was cool. 'You can get the same effect from two martinis on an empty stomach.'

She was unperturbed. 'No, you can't, Edward,' she said. 'You cannot.'

They were silent again for several miles. Past the plant the road broadened for a while and became straighter. Edward speeded up. It was late and he was getting bored. The grass's singing had become quieter. He was focusing on the road when he heard a sharp intake of breath from Myra and then he saw that somehow there was more light on the road. And Myra said softly, 'The *rings*, Edward,' and he looked up and there they were: the lavender and pale blue rings of Belsin. Normally invisible but now glowing in a great arc from east to west above them. Fairy rings. Rings of heaven.

The grass seemed to crescendo for a moment, in some kind of coda, and then became silent. The rings brightened. The effect was stunning.

'Stop the jeep,' Myra said. 'Let's look.'

'Haven't time,' Edward said, and drove on.

And Myra did something she had never done before because of the pain her unlucky body could cause her: she pushed the lever on her seat and leaned in it all the way back and looked up at the beautiful rings in the sky. She did it with care and lay back and relaxed, still holding her unfinished drink, now in her lap. Her dark hair blew behind her in the jeep's wind. Edward could see by the light of the rings that her face was glowing. Her body looked light, supple, youthful in the light. Her smile was beatific.

He noticed the unfinished drink. 'God,' he thought, 'she may be getting well.'

The orchids grew down the sides of the only cliffs on Belsin. Belsin was a nearly flat planet with almost nothing to fall from. That, and the low gravity, made it a very safe place, as Edward had noted early in his life there.

The orchids were not orchids, were not even plants, but they looked somewhat like orchids. They were the outward flowerings of some obscure life form that, like the grass, seemed to go down to the center of the planet. You could not uproot an orchid any more than you could pull a blade of the grass loose from the surface; a thin but incredibly tenuous filament at the base of them went through solid obsidian down to a depth far below possible exploration or investigation. They were stunningly beautiful to see.

They glowed in shades of green and yellow with waving plumes and leaves shaped like enormous Japanese fans. They were both luminous and illuminated and they shifted as they moved from transparent to translucent to opaque.

When he stopped the jeep near the orchid cliffs, he heard a small cry from Myra and looked over to see her features in the familiar grimace of pain; riding that way had almost certainly been too much for her, even with Endolin.

Yet she sat up easily enough, though very slowly, and got out of the jeep. He did not offer to help; she had told him years before that she preferred doing things by herself when she could. By the time she was standing she was smiling again. As he came around to her side of the jeep he saw her casually emptying her drink on the ground at her feet, where it made several pools in the obsidian. She set the glass in the jeep.

They walked forward slowly. Both wore gum-rubber soles on their shoes, but the surface could be treacherous. She appeared to have recovered from the pain in the jeep; her walking was as certain as his own. Possibly steadier. 'Myra,' he said, 'I think you're getting better.' His voice was flat.

'It would be really something, Edward, not to be just a sick rich girl. To be able to do something besides lie around and take pills and try to get around the pain. It would be great to *work*.'

'Work?' he said. 'At what?'

'I don't know,' she said. 'At anything. I could learn to be a pilot, or a librarian. You know, Edward, I'm not terribly smart. I think I could be very happy doing housework. Having children. Just being *busy* for the rest of my life, instead of living in my mind all the time.'

'It's good to see you thinking about it,' he said. But it wasn't. He hated the whole idea. A sick Myra was bad enough; he did not want this chipper, nearly well one around to clutter up his life.

And the more well she became the harder it would be to kill her and to blame her death on the arthritis.

He looked toward the orchid observation platform. There was another couple standing there, and as they came closer Edward could see that the man was an engineer named Strang – one of the steadier, more reliable people from the plant. The girl was somebody from Accounting.

And it began to shape up for him then. The situation was really good. He had long suspected that the orchid cliffs were the best place for it. And here were the perfect witnesses. It was dark and everyone knew the orchid cliffs were dangerous at night. Myra had been drinking; the autopsy would show that.

It began to click off for him the way things did sometimes. He embellished it. As they approached the other couple enough to be overheard he said, 'Myra, it's really strange of you to want to come out here like this. Maybe we shouldn't go to the cliffs. We can come back in daylight tomorrow . . .'

She laughed in a way that he hoped would sound drunken and said, 'Oh, come on, Edward. I feel marvelous.'

'Okay, darling. Anything you say.' He spoke to her lovingly and then looked up to greet the other couple.

'Nice seeing you, Mr MacDonnell,' the engineer said 'The orchids are really fine by ringlight.'

'I'd still rather be in bed,' Edward said amiably. 'Bu Mrs MacDonnell wanted to come out here. She says sh could dance till dawn.'

Myra beamed at Strang and Strang and his girl nodded politely at her. Myra never saw people on Belsin. Arthriti had made her life sedentary, and even though Belsin had relieved the pain greatly she had never learned to b sociable. Most of her time was spent reading, listening to music, or puttering around the house.

'More power to you, Mrs MacDonnell,' Strang said And then, as they went out on the ledge toward th staircase, 'Careful out there, you two!'

There was a meandering walkway, partly carved from obsidian, partly constructed from moonwood, that ra along the cliff face toward a high waterfall. The steps wer lighted by hidden electric lights and there was sti ringlight from above. There was a safety rail, too, o heavy moonwood, waist high. But it was only a handra and a person could slip under it. The thing could hav been done better, but there was only so much huma labor available on the planet for projects of that kind

The two of them went slowly along the staircase, still i view of Strang and his girl. The light on the orchids wa gorgeous. They could hear the sound of the waterfall. I was very cool. Myra was becoming excited. 'My God,' sh said, 'Belsin is really a lovely place. With the grass tha sings, and the orchids.' She looked up at the sky. 'An those rings.'

'Watch your step,' he said. He looked back at Stran and waved. Then they went around the edge of a cliff, an along a wet obsidian wall where the light glared off th wetness and was for a moment almost blinding. For a instant he thought of pushing her off there, but they we too close to Strang: if there were a struggle it might t heard. They walked along a level place for a while. My would look across at the orchids on the other side, wi their fans gently changing color in the night air and wou gasp at the beauty of them. Sometimes she squeezed his arm strongly or hugged him in her excitement. He knew it was all beautiful, but it had never really touched him and it certainly wasn't touching him now. He was thinking coolly of the best way to kill Myra. And some part of him was second-guessing, thinking that it might not be bad to go on living with Myra if she got well, that it was cruel to think of killing her just when she was beginning to enjoy her life. But then he thought of her dumbness, of her innocence. He thought of her money.

Suddenly they came around a turn in the walkway and there was the waterfall. Part of it reflected the colors of the rings above. There was spray on his face. He looked down. Just ahead of them was a place where the obsidian was wet. The moonwood railing had been doubled at that point but there was still a distance of at least two feet from the bottom where a person could easily slip under. He looked farther down – straight down. The chasm was half a mile – the highest drop on Belsin.

He looked behind him. They could not be seen. *Okay*, he thought. *Best to be quick about it.*

He took her firmly by the arm, put his free arm around her waist.

She turned and looked at his face. Hers was calm, open. 'You're going to kill me. Aren't you, Edward?' she said.

'That's right,' he said. 'I didn't think you knew.'

'Oh, I knew all right,' she said.

For a moment he was frightened. 'Have you told anyone? Written anyone?'

'No.'

'That's stupid of you. To tell me that. You could have lied.'

'Maybe,' she said. 'But Edward, a part of me has always wanted to die. My kind of life is hardly worth the effort. I'm not sure that getting well would change that either.'

They stood there like that by the waterfall for a full several minutes. He had her gripped firmly. It would only be a matter of putting one of his feet behind hers, tripping her and pushing her under the railing. She looked very

113

calm and yet not passive. His heart was beating furiously. His skin seemed extraordinarily sensitive; he felt each drop of spray as it hit. The waterfall sounded very loud.

He stared down at her. She looked pathetic. 'Aren't you frightened?' he said.

She did not speak for a moment. Then she said, 'Yes. I'm frightened, Edward. But I'm not terrified.'

He had to admit that. She was taking it very well. 'Would you rather jump?' he said. He could let go of her. There was no way she could outrun him. And he wanted no bruises from his hands on her arms, no shoe mark of his on her legs. Her body – what was left of her body – would be studied by the best criminologists from Earth; he could be sure her family would see to that. She'd be kept frozen in orbit until the experts got there.

Thinking of that, he looked up toward the sky. The rings had begun to fade. 'No,' Myra said. 'I can't jump. It's too frightening. You'll have to push me.'

'All right,' he said, looking back to her.

'Edward,' she said. 'Please don't hurt me. I've always hated pain.'

Those were her last words. She did not fight back. When he pushed her off she fell silently, in the low gravity, for a long, long time before smashing herself on the obsidian at the bottom of the chasm.

As he looked up the rings appeared again, but only for a moment.

Getting her out with a helicopter and then making the statement and getting Strang and his girl to make their statements took all night. There was no police force and no 'law' as such on Belsin, but the factory manager was Acting Magistrate and took testimony. Everyone appeared to believe Edward's story – that Myra was drunk and slipped – and condolences were given. Her body was put in a plastic capsule from a supply that had sat idle for years; she was the first person ever to die on Belsin.

Edward drove back at daybreak. His fatigue was enormous but his mind was calm. He had almost begun to believe the story himself.

As he approached the now empty house across the broad plain a remarkable thing began to happen: the grass began to sing again. Belsin grass was only known to sing in the evening. Never at dawn. But there it was singing as the first of the planet's two suns was coming up. And somehow – perhaps because of the clarity in the fatigue he felt – it seemed to him that the grass's song was almost comprehensible. It seemed to be singing to him alone.

He spent half of the next day sleeping and the other half of it sitting in various rooms of the house, drinking gin. He did not miss Myra, nor did he feel guilty, nor apprehensive. He thought for a while, half-drunkenly, about what he would do, back on Earth as a rich, single man. He was still under forty; if he was lucky he would begin to inherit some of Myra's millions within a year.

There were still a few things to decide upon now and as he drank he thought about them from time to time: should he continue running the Endolin plant while waiting for the inquest into Myra's death and for the ship that would take him back to Earth? If not, there was very little else to do on Belsin. He could spend some time exploring down south, where the obsidian was a light gray and where no Endolin had been found. He could sit around the house drinking, listen to some of Myra's records, watch TV from the tape library, work out in the basement gym. None of it really appealed to him and he began to fear the dullness of the wait. He wanted to be on Earth right now, at the heart of things, with bright lights, and variety and speed and money. He wanted his life to start moving fast. He wanted travel: loose and easy nights on gamier planets with well-dressed women, guitars playing. He wanted to buy new clothes on Earth, take an apartment in Venice, go to the races in the Bois de Boulogne. Then see the galaxy in style.

And then, as twilight came, he moved out onto the terrace to watch the setting of the second of Belsin's two small suns, and realized that the grass was singing again.

Its sound was very faint; at first he thought it was only a ringing in his ears. He walked, drink in hand, to the railing at the end of the big moonwood terrace, walking softly in bare feet across the silvery surface, cool as always to the touch. Belsin, bare and nearly devoid of life as it was, could be – as Myra would say – lovely. He remembered Myra's falling, then, as in a dream. At one-half Earth gravity her body had fallen away from him slowly, slowly decreasing its size as it had lazily spun. She had not screamed. Her dress had fluttered upward in his direction as he stood there with his hands lightly on the wet railing of the Orchid Chasm.

Suddenly and surprisingly he began to see it from her falling-away point of view; looking up at himself standing there diminishing in size, seeing his own set features, his tan cotton shirt, blue jeans, his rumpled brown hair. His cold unblinking eyes looking down on himself, falling.

The grass was not really singing. It was talking. Whispering. For a shocked moment it seemed to him that it whispered, 'Edward. Edward.' And then, as he turned to go back into the house for another drink, 'Myra is here Edward, Myra is here.'

Another very strong drink put him to sleep. He dreamed of himself in lines of people, waiting. Long confusing lines at a cafeteria or a theater, with silent people and he among them also silent, impatient, trapped in an endless waiting. And he awoke sweating, wide awake in the middle of the Belsin night. Before his open eyes Myra fell, at a great distance from him now, slowly spinning. He could hear the sound of the waterfall. He sat up. He was still wearing his blue jeans.

It was not the waterfall; what he heard was the grass whispering to him.

He pushed open the bedroom window. The grass was clearer now. Its voice was clearly speaking his name 'Edward,' it said. 'Edward. Edward.'

Into his mind leaped the words from the old poem studied in college:

116

> Why does your sword so drip wi' blood
> Edward, Edward?

The fuzziness of liquor had left him. His head was preternaturally clear. 'What do you want?' he said.

'I want to talk,' the grass said. Its voice was lazy, sleepy.

'Can't you be heard everywhere?'

'Do you fear overhearing?' The voice was fairly clear, although soft.

'Yes.'

'I'm only speaking near the house.' That was what he thought it said. The words were a bit blurred toward the end of the sentence.

'Near the house?' He pulled the window open wider. Moved closer. Then he sat on the edge of the bed by the window and leaned out into the night. Two small moons were up and he could see the grass. It seemed to be rippling, as though a slight, thin-aired wind were stroking it. The grass grew about two feet high and was normally a pale brown. The moonlight was like Earth moonlight; it made it look silver, the color of moonwood. He sat with his hands on his upper thighs, his bare feet on the floor carpeting, listening to the grass.

'Near the house, Edward,' the grass said.

'And you're Myra?'

'Oh, yes, I'm Myra.' There was a tone of gaiety in this, a hushed joyfulness in the whispering. 'I'm Myra and I'm Belsin. I've become this planet, Edward.'

'Jesus Christ!' he said. 'I need a drink. And a cigarette.'

'The cigarettes are in the kitchen cabinet,' the grass said. 'Come out on the terrace when you get them. I want to see you.'

'See me?' he said.

'I can see with my rings,' the voice said. Myra said.

He got up and padded into the kitchen. Strangely he did not feel agitated. He was on some ledge somewhere in the middle of the quiet night, hung over and a wife-murderer, yet his soul was calm. He found the cigarettes easily,

117

opened them, took one out and lit it. He poured a small amount of gin into a glass, filled it the rest of the way with orange juice, thinking as he did so of how far a distance from California that juice had come, to be drunk by him here in this steel kitchen in the middle of the night on a planet where the grass had become his wife. The whole planet was his wife. His ex-wife. He drank a swallow from the glass, after swishing it around to mix the gin in. The glow from it in his stomach was warm and mystical. He walked slowly, carrying his glass and his cigarette, out to the terrace.

'Ooooh!' the grass said. 'I can see you now.'

He looked up to the sky. 'I don't see the rings,' he said. 'Your rings.'

And then they appeared. Glowing pink and lavender, clearly outlined against the dim-lit sky. They disappeared.

'I'm only learning to show my rings,' Myra said. 'I have to thicken the air in the right place, so the light bends downward toward you.' There was silence for a while. The grass had become clearer when it last spoke. It spoke again finally and was clearer still, so that it almost seemed as if Myra were sitting on the terrace next to him, her soft voice perfectly audible in the silent night. 'There's a lot to learn, Edward.'

He drank again. 'How did it happen?' And then, almost blurting it out, 'Are you going to tell people about what I did?'

'Goodness, Edward, I hadn't thought about that.' The voice paused. 'Right now I don't know.'

He felt relieved. Myra had always been good-hearted despite the self-pity. She usually gave the benefit of the doubt.

He sat silent for a while, looking at the vast plain in front of his eyes, concentrating on his drink. Then he said, 'You didn't answer me, Myra. About how it happened.'

'I know,' the grass said. 'I know I didn't. Edward, I'm not only Myra, I'm Belsin too. I am this planet and I'm learning to be what I have become.' There was no self-pity in that, no complaint. She was speaking to him clearly

118

trying to tell him something.

'What I know is that Belsin wanted an ego. Belsin wanted someone to die here. Before I died and was . . . was taken in, Belsin could not speak in English. My grass could only speak to the feelings of people but not to their minds.'

'The singing?' he said.

'Yes. I learned singing when Captain Belsin first landed. He carried a little tape player with him as he explored and played music on it. The grass learned . . . I learned to sing. He had headaches and took aspirin for them and I learned to make Endolin for him. But he never used it. Never discovered it.' The voice was wistful, remembering something unpleasant. 'I couldn't talk then. I could only feel some of the things that people felt. I could feel what happened to Captain Belsin's headache when he took aspirin and I knew how to improve on it. But I couldn't tell him to use it. That was found out later.' The grass rippled and was still. It was darker now; one of the moons had set while they were talking.

'Can you bring up some more moons? So I can see you better? See the grass?' There were four moons.

'I'll try,' Myra said. There was silence. Nothing happened. Finally Myra said, 'No, I can't. I can't change their orbits.'

'Thanks for trying,' he said dryly. 'The first person to die here would become the planet? Or merge with its mind? Is that it?'

'I think so,' Myra said. He thought he could see a faint ripple on the word 'think.' 'I became reincarnated as Belsin. Remember the rings lighting after you pushed me over?'

'Yes.'

'I was waking up then. It was really splendid for me. To wake into this body. Edward,' she said, 'I'm so alive now, and vigorous. *And nothing about me hurts.*'

He looked away, back toward the silent house. Then he finished his drink. Myra's voice had been strong, cheerful. He had been calm – or had been *acting* calm – but something in his deep self was disturbed. He was becoming uneasy about all this. Talking with the grass did not disturb him. He was a realist, and if grass could talk to him in the voice of his dead wife he would hold conversation with grass. And Myra, clearly, wasn't dead – although her old, arthritic body certainly was. He had seen it as they brought it in from the helicopter; even in low gravity, falling onto jagged obsidian could lacerate and spatter.

'Do you hate me for what I did?' he said, fishing.

'No, Edward. Not at all. I feel . . . removed from you. But then I really always did. I always knew that you only allowed a small part of yourself to touch my life. And now,' she said, 'my life is bigger and more exciting. And I only need a small part of you.'

That troubled him, sent a little line of fear across a ridge somewhere in his stomach. It took him a moment to realize that it was her word 'need' that had frightened him.

'Why do you need me, Myra?' he said, carefully.

'To read to me.'

He stared. 'To read to you?'

'Yes, Edward. I want you to read from our library.' They had brought several thousand books on microfilm with them. 'And I'll want you to play records for me.'

'My God!' he said. 'Doesn't a whole planet have better things to do?'

The grass seemed to laugh. 'Of course. Of course I have things to do. Just getting to know this body of mine. And I can sense that I am in touch with others – others like the Belsin part of me. Now that I have an ego – Myra's ego – I can converse with them. Feel their feelings.'

'Well then,' he said, somewhat relieved.

'Yes,' she said. 'But I'm still Myra, too. And I want to read. And I want music – honest, old-fashioned Earth music. I have this wonderful new body, Edward, but I don't have hands. I can't turn pages or change records, And I'll need you to talk to, from time to time. As long as I remain human. Or half human.'

Jesus Christ! he thought silently. But then he began to think that if she had no hands, even needed him to run microfilm, that she could not stop him from leaving. She was only a voice, and rings, and ripples in the grass. What could she do? She couldn't alter the orbits of her moons.

'What about the other people here on Belsin?' he said, still careful with his words. 'One of them might want to read to you. A younger man, maybe . . .'

This time her laughter was clearly laughter. 'Oh no, Edward,' she said. 'I don't want them. It's you I want.' There was silence for several long moments. Then she continued, 'They'll be going back to Earth in a few months anyway. I've stopped making Endolin.'

'Stopped . . . ?'

'When you were asleep. I was planning things then. I realized that if I stopped Endolin they would all go away.'

'What about all those people on Earth who need it?' he said, trying to play on her sympathies. He did not give a damn, himself, for the pains of other people. That was why living with Myra had not really been difficult for him.

'They'll be making it synthetically before the supplies run out,' she said. 'It's difficult, but they'll learn. It would make people rich to find out how. Money motivates some people strongly.'

He said nothing to that except 'Excuse me' and got up and went into the kitchen for another drink. The sky was lightening; the first little sun would be up soon. He had never known Myra to think as clearly as she could think now. He shuddered and poured himself a bigger drink. Then, through the terrace doors, he heard her voice. 'Come on back out, Edward.'

'Oh, shut up!' he said and went over and slammed the doors shut and locked them. It was triply thick glass and the room became silent. He walked into the living room, with its brown-enameled steel walls and brown carpet and the oil paintings and Shaker furniture. He could hear the grass from the windows in there, so he closed them and pulled the thick curtains over them. It was silent. 'Christ!' he said aloud and sat down with his drink to think about it.

121

Myra kept several antique plates on little shelves over the television set. They were beginning to vibrate. And then, shockingly, he heard a deep bass rumbling and the plates fell to the floor and broke. The rumbling continued for a moment before he realized that it had been an earthquake. He was suddenly furious and he hung on to the fury, covering up the fear that had come with it. He got up and went through the kitchen to the terrace doors, flung them open into the still night. 'For Christ's sake, Myra,' he said, 'what are you trying to do?'

'That was a selective tremor,' the grass said. There was a hint of coyness in its tone. 'I pushed magma toward the house and let a fissure fall. Just a tiny bit, Edward. Hardly any at all.'

'It could have fallen farther?' he said, trying to keep the anger and the sternness in his voice.

'Lord, yes,' Myra said. 'That was only about half on the Richter scale.' He suddenly remembered that Myra had studied geology at Ohio State; she was well prepared to become a planet. 'I'm pretty sure I could go past ten. With hardly any practice.'

'Are you threatening to earthquake me into submission?'

She didn't answer for a minute. Then she said, pleasantly, 'I want to keep you here with me, Edward. We're married. And I need you.'

The earthquake had been frightening. But he thought of the supply ships and of the ship that would be bringing the people for the inquest. All he would have to do would be to lie to her, act submissive, and then somehow get on board the ship and away from Belsin before she earthquaked.

'And you want me to read aloud? Or run the microfilm for you?'

'Aloud, Edward,' she said. 'I'll let the others leave, but I want you to stay here. Here in the house.'

'I'll have to get out every now and then.'

'No, you won't,' Myra said.

'I'll need food.'

'I'm already growing it for you. The trees will be up in a few days. And the vegetables: carrots and potatoes and beans and lettuce. Even tobacco, Edward. But no liquor. You'll have to do without liquor once the supply is gone. But this place will be *lovely*. I'll have a lake for you and groves of fruit trees. I can grow anything – the way I grew Endolin before. This will be a beautiful place for you, Edward. A real Eden. And you'll have it all to yourself.'

He thought crazily of Venice, of women, guitar music. Venice and Rome. Panicked suddenly, he said, 'I can run away with the others. You can't earthquake us all to death. That would be cruel . . .'

'That's true enough,' Myra said. 'But if you leave this house I'll open a fissure under you and down you'll go.' She paused a long moment. 'Just like I did, Edward. Down and down.'

He began to talk faster, louder. 'What if they come to take me away, to force me to go back to Earth?'

'Oh, come on, Edward. Quit it. I won't let them ever get to the house. They'll go away eventually. And I'll never let anyone land again. Just swallow them up if they try it.'

He felt terribly weary. He walked out onto the terrace and slumped onto the moonwood bench. Myra remained silent. He had nothing to say. He sipped his drink, letting his mind go blank. He sat there alone for a half hour. Or not really alone. It was beginning to dawn on him that he might never be alone again.

Then Myra spoke again, softly. 'I know you're tired, Edward. But I don't sleep. Not anymore. I wonder if you would read to me a while. I was in the middle of *The King's Mistress*. If you'll switch the microfilm machine on you'll find my page.'

'Christ!' he said, startled. 'You can't *make* me read.' There was something petulant in his voice. He could hear it and it disturbed him. Something of the sound of a small boy trying to defy his mother. 'I want to have another drink and go back to bed.'

'You know I don't like insisting,' Myra said. 'And you're

perfectly right, Edward. I can't make you read. But I can shake the house and keep you awake.' Abruptly the house shook from another tremor, probably a quarter of a point on the Richter scale. 'And,' Myra said, 'I can grow food for you or not grow food for you. And I can give you what you want to eat or not give you what you want. I could feed you nothing but persimmons for a few months. And make the water taste terrible.'

'Jesus Christ!' he said. 'I'm *tired*.'

'It'll only be a couple of chapters,' Myra said. 'And then maybe a couple of old songs on the player, and I'll go back to contemplating my interior and the other planets around here.'

He didn't move.

'You'll be wanting me to grow tobacco for you. There are only a few cartons of cigarettes left.' Edward smoked three packs a day. Three packs in a short Belsin day.

He still didn't move.

'Well,' Myra said, conciliatory now. 'I think I could synthesize a little ethyl alcohol. If I could do Endolin, I suppose I could do that too. Maybe a quart or so every now and then. A hundred ninety proof.'

He stood up. He was terribly weary. '*The King's Mistress*?' he said.

'That's right!' the grass said, sweetly, joyfully. 'I've always liked your voice, Edward. It'll be good to hear you read.'

And then, before he turned to go into the house, to the big console that held thousands of books – thousands of dumb Gothic novels and books on gardening and cooking and self-improvement and a few technical books on geology – he saw everything get suddenly much lighter and looked up to see that the great rings of Belsin were now fully visible, bright as bands of sunlight in the abruptly brightened sky above his head. They glowed in full realization of themselves, illuminating the whole, nearly empty planet.

And Myra's voice came sighing joyfully in a great, horizon ripple of grass. 'Ooooooh!' it said happily. 'Oooooooh!'

Out of Luck

It was only three months after he had left his wife and children and moved in with Janet that Janet decided she had to go to Washington for a week. Harold was devastated. He tried not to let her see it. The fiction between them was that he had left Gwen so he could grow up, change his life and learn to paint again. But all he was certain of was that he had left Gwen to have Janet as his mistress. There were other reasons: his recovery from alcoholism, the years he had wasted his talent as an art professor, and Gwen's refusal to move to New York with him. But none of these would have been sufficient to uproot him and cause him to take a year's leave from his job if Janet had not worn peach-colored bikini panties that stretched tightly across her lovely ass.

He spent the morning after she left cleaning up the kitchen and washing the big pot with burned zucchini in it. Janet had made him three quarts of zucchini soup before leaving on the shuttle, along with two jars of chutney, veal stew in a blue casserole dish, and two loaves of Irish soda bread. It was very international. The mess in the tiny kitchen of her apartment took him two hours to clean up. Then he cooked himself a breakfast of scrambled eggs and last night's mashed potatoes, fried with onions. He drank two cups of coffee from Janet's Chemex. Drinking the coffee, he walked several times into the living room where his easel stood and looked at the quarter-done painting. Each time he looked at it his heart sank. He did not want to finish the painting – not that painting, that dumb, academic abstraction. But there was no other painting for him to paint right now. What he wanted was Janet.

Janet was a very successful folk art dealer. They had met at a museum party. She was in Washington now as a consultant to the National Gallery. She had said to him, 'No, I don't think you should come to Washington with me. We need to be apart from each other for a while. I'm beginning to feel suffocated.' He had nodded sagely while his heart sank.

One problem was that he distrusted folk art and Janet's interest in it, the way he distrusted Janet's fondness for her cats. Janet talked to her cats a lot. He was neutral about cats themselves, but he felt people who talked to them were trivial. And being interested in badly painted nineteenth-century portraits also seemed trivial to him now.

He looked at the two gold-framed American primitives above Janet's sofa, said, 'Horseshit!' and drew back his mug in a fantasy of throwing coffee on them both.

Across from the apartment, on Sixty-third Street, workmen were renovating an old mansion; they had been at it three months before, when Harold had moved in. He watched them for a minute now, mixing cement in a wheelbarrow, and bringing sacks of it from a truck at the corner of Madison Avenue. Three workmen in white undershirts held sunlit discourse on the plywood ramp that had replaced the building's front steps. Behind windows devoid of glass he could see men moving back and forth. But nothing happened; nothing seemed to change in the building. It was the same mess it had been before, like his own spiritual growth: lots of noise and movement and no change.

He looked at his watch, relieved. It was ten-thirty. The morning was half over and he needed to go to the bank. He put on a light jacket and left.

As he was waiting in a crowd at the Third Avenue light he heard a voice shout 'Taxi!' and a man pushed roughly past him, right arm high and waving, onto the avenue. The man was about thirty, in faded blue jeans and a sleeveless sweater. A taxi squealed to a stop at the corner and the man conferred with the driver for a moment before getting in. He seemed to be quietly arrogant, preoccupied with something. Harold could have kicked him in the ass. He did not like the man's look of confidence. He did not like his sandy, uncombed hair.

The light changed and the cab took off fast, up Third Avenue.

Harold crossed and went into the bank. He went to a table, quickly made out a check to cash for a hundred, then walked over toward the line. Halfway across the lobby, he stopped cold. The man in the sleeveless sweater was standing in line, holding a checkbook. His lips were pursed in silent whistling. He was wearing the same faded blue jeans and – Harold now noticed – Adidas.

He was looking idly in Harold's direction. Harold averted his eyes. There were at least ten other people waiting behind the man. He had to have been here awhile. An identical twin? A mild hallucination, making two similar people look exactly alike? Harold got in line. After a while the man did his business and left. Harold cashed his check and left, stuffing five twenties into his billfold. Another drain on the seven thousand he had left Michigan with. He had seven thousand to live on for a year in New York, with Janet, while he learned to paint again, to be the self-supporting artist his whiskey dreams had been filled with. Whiskey had left him sitting behind closed suburban blinds at two in the afternoon, reading the J. C. Penney catalog and waiting for Gwen to come home from work. Well. He had been free of whiskey for a year and a half now. First the hospital, then AA.; now New York and Janet.

He walked back toward her apartment, thinking of how his entire bankroll of seven thousand could not pay Janet's rent for three months. And she had taken this big New York place after two years of living in an even larger apartment in Paris. On a marble-topped lingerie chest in one of the bathrooms was a snapshot of her, astride a gleaming Honda, on the Boulevard des Capucines by the ironwork doorway of that apartment. When that photograph was taken Harold had been living in a ranch house in Michigan and was driving a Chevrolet.

He glanced down Park Avenue while crossing it and

saw a sleeveless sweater and faded jeans, from the back, disappearing into one of the tall apartment buildings. He shuddered and quickened his pace. He shifted his billfold from a rear to a front pocket, picturing those pickpockets who bump you from behind and rob you while apologizing, on the streets of New York. His mother – his very protective mother – had told him about that twenty years before. Part of him loved New York, loved its action and its anonymity, along with the food and clothes and bookstores. Another part of him feared it. The sight of triple locks on apartment doors could frighten him, or of surly Puerto Ricans with well-muscled arms, carrying their big, noisy, arrogant radios. Their kill-the-Anglo radios. The slim-hipped black men frightened him, with long, tight-assed trousers in pale colors, half covering expensive shoes – Italian killer shoes. And there were drunks everywhere. In doorways. Poking studiously through garbage bins for the odd half-eaten pizza slice, the usable worn shirt. Possibly for emeralds and diamonds. Part of him wanted to scrub up a drunk or two, with a Brillo pad, like the zucchini pan. Something satisfying in that.

The man in the sweater had been white, clean, non-menacing. Possibly European. Yet Harold now, crossing Madison, felt chilled by the thought of him. Under the chill was anger. That spoiled, arrogant face, that sandy hair! He hurried back to Janet's apartment building, walked briskly up the stairs to the third floor, let himself in. There in the living room stood the painting. He suddenly saw that it could use a sort of rectangle of pale green, like a distant field of grass, right there. He picked up a brush, very happy to do so. Outside the window, the sun was shining brightly. The workmen on the building were busy. Harold was busy.

He worked for three solid hours and felt wonderful. It was good work too, and the painting was coming along. At last.

For lunch he made himself a bacon and tomato sandwich on toast. It was simple midwestern fare and he loved it.

When he had finished eating, he went back into the living room, sat in the black director's chair in front of the window and looked at the painting by afternoon light. It looked good – just a tad spooky, the way he wanted it to be. It would be a good painting after all. It was really working. He decided to go to a movie.

The movie he wanted to see was called *Out of Luck*. It was a comedy from France, advertised as 'an hilarious sex farce,' with subtitles. It sounded fine for a sunny fall afternoon. He walked down Madison toward the theater.

There were an awful lot of youthful, well-dressed people on Madison Avenue. They probably all spoke French. He looked in the windows of places with names like Le Relais, La Bagagerie, Le Bijou. He would have given ten dollars to see a J. C. Penney's or a plain barber shop with a red and white barber's pole.

As he was crossing Fifty-seventh Street, traffic-snarled as usual, there was suddenly the loud *harrumphing* of a pair of outrageously noisy motorcycles and with a rush of hot air two black Hondas zoomed past him. From the back the riders appeared to be a man and a woman although the sexual difference was hard to detect. Each wore a spherical helmet that reflected the sun; the man's helmet was red, the other green. Science fiction helmets; they hurt the eyes with reflected and dazzling sunlight. There was a smell of exhaust. Each of the riders, man and woman, was wearing a brown sleeveless sweater and blue jeans. Each wore Adidas over white socks. Their shirts were short-sleeved, blue. So had been the shirts of the man in the taxi and the man in line at Chemical Bank. Harold's stomach twisted. He wanted to scream.

The cyclists disappeared in traffic, darting into it with insouciance, tilting their black bikes first this way and then that, as though merely leaning their way through the congestion of taxies and limousines and sanitation trucks.

Maybe it was a fad in dress. Maybe coincidence. He had never noticed before how many people wore brown sleeveless sweaters. Who counted such things? And

130

everyone wore jeans. He was wearing jeans himself.

The movie was at Fifty-seventh and Third. The theater had only a scattering of people in it, since it was the middle of the afternoon. The story was about a woman who was haunted by the gravelly voice of her dead lover – a younger man who had been killed in a motorcycle accident. She was a gorgeous woman and went through a sequence of affairs, breaking up with each new lover after the voice of her old, dead one pointed out their flaws to her, or distracted her while making love. It really was funny. Sometimes, though, it made Harold edgy, when he thought of the young lover Janet had had before him, who had disappeared from her life in some way he, Harold, did not know about. But several times he laughed loudly.

And then, toward the end of the movie, her lover reappeared, apparently not dead at all. It was on a quiet Paris street. She was out walking with an older man she had just slept with, going to buy some coffee, when a black Honda pulled up to the curb beside her. She stopped. The driver pulled off his helmet. Harold's heart almost stopped beating and he stared crazily. There in front of him, on the Cinemascope movie screen, was the huge image of a youngish man with sandy hair, a brown sleeveless sweater, blue shirt, Adidas. The man smiled at the woman. She collapsed in a faint.

When the man on the motorcycle spoke, his voice was as it had been when it was haunting her: gravelly and bland. Harold wanted to throw something at the screen, wanted to scream at the image, 'Get out of here, you arrogant fucker!' But he did nothing and said nothing. He stayed in his seat, waiting for the movie to end. It ended with the woman getting on the dead lover's motorcycle and riding off with him. He wouldn't tell her where he lived now. He was going to show her.

Harold watched the credits closely, wanting to find the actor who had played the old lover. His name in the film had been Paul. But no actor was listed for the name of Paul. The others were there, but not Paul. *What in God's name is happening?* Harold thought. He left the theater

131

and, hardly daring to look around himself on the bright street, flagged down a cab and went home. Could a person hallucinate a character into a movie? Was the man at the bank in fact a French movie actor? Twelve years of drinking could fuck up your brain chemistry pretty badly. But he hadn't even had the DTs. His New York psychiatrist had told him he was badly regressed at times, but his sanity had never been in question.

In the apartment he was able, astonishingly, to get back into the painting for a few hours. He made a few changes, making it spookier. *He* felt spookier now and it came out onto the canvas. The painting was nearly done. When he stopped, it was eight o'clock in the evening. The workmen across the street had finished their day hours before. They had packed up their tools and had gone home to Queens or wherever. The building, as always, was unchanged; its doorways and windows gaped blankly. There was a pile of rubble by the plywood entry platform where there had always been a pile of rubble.

He went into the kitchen, ignored the veal stew Janet had made for him and lit the oven. Then he took a Hungry Man chicken pie out of the freezer, ripped off the cardboard box, stabbed the frozen top crust a few times with her Sabatier, slipped it into the oven and set the timer for forty-five minutes.

He went back into the living room, looked again at the painting. 'Maybe I needed the shit scared out of me,' he said aloud. But the thought of the man in the sweater chilled him. He went over to the hutch in the corner, opened its left door, flipped on the little Sony TV inside. Then he crossed the big room to the dry sink and began rummaging for candy. He kept candy in various places.

He found a couple of pieces of butterscotch and began sucking on one of them. Back in the kitchen he opened the oven door a moment, enjoying the feel of the hot air. His little Hungry Man pie sat inside, waiting for him.

There had been a man's voice on television for a minute or so, reciting some kind of disaster news. A California brush fire or something. There in the kitchen Harold began to realize that the voice was familiar, gravelly. It had a slight French accent. He rushed into the living room, still holding a potholder. On the TV screen was the sandy-haired man in the sweater, saying '... from Pasadena, California, for NBC news.' Then John Chancellor came on.

Harold threw the potholder at the TV screen. 'You son of a bitch!' he shouted. 'You ubiquitous son of a bitch!' Then he sank into the director's chair, on the edge of tears. His eyes burned.

It was dark outside when his pie was ready. He ate it as if it were cardboard, forcing himself to eat every bite. To keep his strength up, as his mother would have said, for the oncoming storm. For the oncoming storm.

He kept the TV off that evening and did not go out. He finished the painting by artificial light at three in the morning, took two Sominex tablets and went to bed, frightened. He had wanted to call Janet but hadn't. That would have been chicken. He slept without dreaming for nine hours.

It was noon when he got up from the big platform bed and stumbled into the kitchen for breakfast. He drank a cup of cold zucchini soup while waiting for the coffee from yesterday to heat up. He felt okay, ready for the man in the sweater whenever he might strike. The coffee boiled over, spattering the white wall with brown tears. He reached to pull the big Chemex off the burner and scalded himself. 'Shit!' he said, and held his burned hand under cold tapwater for a half minute. He walked into the living room and began looking at the painting in daylight. It was really very good. Just the right feeling, the right arrangement. Scary, too. He took it from the easel, set it against a wall. Then he thought better of that. The cats might get at it. He hadn't seen the cats for a while. He looked around him. No cats. He put the painting on top of the dry sink, out of harm's way. He would put out some cat food.

From outside came the sound of a motorcycle. Or of

two motorcycles. He turned, looked out the window. There was dust where the motorcycles had just been, a light cloud of it settling. On the plywood platform at the entryway to the building being renovated stood two men in brown sleeveless sweaters, blue shirts, jeans. One was holding a clipboard, and they were talking. He could not hear their voices even though the window was open. He walked slowly to the window, placed his hands on the ledge, stared down at them. He stared at the same sandy hair, the same face. Two schoolgirls in plaid skirts walked by, on their way to lunch. Behind them was a woman in a brown sleeveless sweater and blue jeans, with sandy hair. She had the same face as the man, only slightly feminized in the way the head set on the shoulders. And she walked like a woman. She walked by the two men, her twins, ignoring them.

Harold looked at his watch. Twelve-fifteen. His heart was pounding painfully. He went to the telephone and called his psychiatrist. It was lunch hour and he might be able to reach him. He did, for a minute or two. Quickly he told him that he was beginning to see the same person everywhere. Even in the movies and on TV. Sometimes two or three at a time.

'What do you think, Harold?' he said to the doctor. The psychiatrist's name was Harold, too.

'It would have to be hallucination. Maybe coincidence.'

'It's not coincidence. There've been seven of them and they are identical, doctor. *Identical*.' His voice, he realized, was not hysterical. It might become that way, he thought, if the doctor should say 'Interesting,' as they do in the movies.

'I'm sorry that you have an hallucination,' Harold the psychiatrist said. 'I wish I could see you this afternoon but I can't. In fact, I have to go now. I have a patient.'

'Harold!' Harold said. 'I've had a dozen sessions with you. Am I the type who hallucinates?'

'No, you aren't, Harold,' the psychiatrist said. 'You really don't seem to me to be like that at all. It's puzzling. Just don't drink.'

'I won't, Harold,' he said, and hung up.

What to do? he thought. *I can stay inside until Janet comes back. I don't have to go out for anything. Maybe it will stop on its own.*

And then he thought, *But so what? They can't hurt me. What if I see a whole bunch of them today? So what? I can ignore them.* He would get dressed and go out. What the hell. Confront the thing.

When he got outdoors, the two of them were gone from in front of the building. He looked to his right, over toward Madison. One of them was just crossing the street, walking lightly on the Adidas. There were ordinary men and women around him. Hell, *he* was ordinary enough. There were just too many of him. Like a clone. Two more crossed, a man and a woman. They were holding hands. Harold decided to walk over to Fifth Avenue.

Just before the corner of Fifth was a wastebasket with a bum poking around in it. Harold had seen this bum before, had given him a quarter once. Fellow alcoholic. There but for the grace of God, et cetera. He fished a quarter from his pocket and gave it to the bum without solicitation. 'Say,' Harold said, on a wild impulse, 'have you noticed something funny? People in brown sweaters and jeans?' He felt foolish, asking. The bum was fragrant in the afternoon sun.

'Hell, yes, buddy,' the bum said. 'Kind of light brown hair? And tennis shoes? Hell yes, they're all over the place.' He shook his head dazedly. 'Can't get no money out of 'em. Tried 'em six, eight times. You got another one of those quarters?'

Harold gave him a dollar. 'Get yourself a drink,' he said.

The bum widened his eyes and took the money silently. He turned to go.

'Hey!' Harold said, calling him back. 'Have a drink for me, will you? I don't drink, myself.' He held out another dollar.

'That's the ticket,' the bum said, carefully, as if addressing a madman. He took the bill quickly, then

135

turned toward Fifth Avenue. 'Hey!' he said. 'There's one of 'em,' and pointed. The man in the brown sleeveless sweater went by, jogging slowly on his Adidas. The bum jammed his two dollars into a pocket and moved on.

Well, the bum had been right. Don't let them interfere with business. But it wasn't hallucination – not unless he had hallucinated the bum and the conversation with the bum. He checked his billfold and found the two dollars were indeed gone. Where would they have gone if he had made up the bum in his unconscious? He hadn't eaten them. If he had, the whole game was over anyway and he was really in a straitjacket somewhere, being fed intravenously, while somebody took notes. Well.

He turned at Fifth Avenue, toward the spire of the Empire State Building, and stopped cold. Most of the foot traffic on the avenue was moving uptown toward him and every third or fourth one of them was the person in the brown sweater and the blue short-sleeved shirt. It was like an invasion from Mars. And he saw that some of the normal people – the people like himself – were staring at them from time to time. The brown-sweatered person was always calm, whistling softly sometimes, cool. The others looked flustered. Harold jammed his hands into his pockets. He felt suddenly cold.

He began walking down Fifth Avenue. He kept going for several blocks, then on an impulse ran across the street to the Central Park side and climbed up on a park bench that faced the avenue and then from the bench onto the stone railing near the Sixtieth Street subway station. He looked downtown, up high now so that he could see. And the farther downtown he looked, the more he saw of an array of brown sweaters, light brown in the afternoon sunlight, with pale, sandy-haired heads above them. On crazy impulse, he looked down at his own clothes and was relieved to see that he was not himself wearing a brown sleeveless sweater and that his jeans were not the pale and faded kind that the person – that the multitude – was wearing.

He got down from the bench and headed across Gran

Army Plaza, past people who were now about one-half sandy-haired and sweatered and the other half just random people. He realized that the repeated person hadn't seemed to crowd the city any more than usual. They weren't *new*, then. If anything, they were replacing the others.

Abruptly, he decided to go into the Plaza Hotel. There were two of them in the lobby, talking quietly with one another, in French. He walked past them toward the Oak Bar; he would get a Perrier in there.

In the bar, three of them sat at the bar itself and two of them were at a table near the front. He seated himself at the bar. A man in a brown sweater turned from where he was washing glasses, wiped his hands on his jeans, came over and said, 'Yes, sir?' The voice was gravelly with a slight French accent, the face blank.

'Perrier with lime,' Harold said. When the man brought it, Harold said, 'How long have you been tending bar here?'

'About twenty minutes,' the man said and smiled.

'Where were you before?'

'Oh, here and there,' the man said. 'You know how it is.'

Harold stared at him, feeling his own face getting red. *No, I don't know how it is!* he said.

The man started to whistle softly. He turned away.

Harold leaned over the bar and took him by the shoulder. The sweater was soft – probably cashmere. Where do you come from? What are you doing?'

The man smiled coldly at him. 'I come from the street. 'm tending bar here.' He stood completely still, waiting or Harold to let go of him.

'Why are there so many of you?' Harold said.

'There's only one of me,' the man said.

'Only one?'

'Just one.' He waited a moment. 'I have to wait on that ouple.' He nodded his head slightly toward the end of the ar. A couple of them had come in, a male and a female as ar as Harold could see in the somewhat dim light.

137

Harold let go of the man, got up and went to a pay telephone on the wall. He dialed his psychiatrist. The phone rang twice and then a male voice said, 'Doctor Morse is not in this afternoon. May I take a message?' The voice was the gravelly voice. Harold hung up. He spun around and faced the bar. The man had just returned from serving drinks to the identical couple at the far end. 'What in hell is your name?' he said, wildly.

The man smiled. 'That's for me to know and you to find out,' he said.

Harold began to cry. 'What's your goddamned *name*? he said, sobbing. 'My name's Harold. For Christ's sake what's yours?'

Now that he was crying, the man looked sympathetic. He turned for a moment to the mirrored shelves behind him, took two unopened bottles of whiskey and then set them on the bar in front of Harold. 'Why don't you just take these, Harold?' he said pleasantly. 'Take them home with you. It's only a few blocks from here.'

'*I'm an alcoholic*,' Harold said, shocked.

'Who cares?' the man said. He got a bright orange shopping bag from somewhere under the bar and put the bottles in it. 'On the house,' he said. Harold stared at him. 'What is your goddamned, fucking *name*?'

'For me to know,' the man said softly. 'For you to find out.'

Harold took the shopping bag, pushed open the door and went into the lobby. There was no doorman at the big doorway of the hotel, but the man in the sleeveless sweater stood there like a doorman. 'Have a good day now, Harold,' the man said as Harold left.

Now there was no one else on the street but the man. Everywhere. And now they all looked at him in recognition, since he had given his name. Their smiles were cool, distant, patronizing. Some nodded at him slightly as he made his way slowly up the avenue toward Sixty-third, some ignored him. Several passed on motorcycles, wearing red helmets. A few waved coolly to him. One slowed his motorcycle down near the curb and said, 'Hi, Harold,' and then sped off. Harold closed his eyes.

He got home all right, and up the stairs. When he walked into the living room he saw that the cats had knocked his new painting to the floor and had badly smeared a corner of it. Apparently one of them had rolled on it. The cats were nowhere in sight. He had not seen them since Janet had gone.

He did not care about the painting now. Not really. He knew what he was going to do. He could see in his mind the French movie, the man on the motorcycle.

In the closet where she kept her vacuum cleaner, Janet also kept a motorcycle helmet. A red one, way up on the top shelf, behind some boxes of candles and light bulbs. She had never spoken to him of motorcycles; he had never asked her about the helmet. He had forgotten it, having noticed it when he was unpacking months before and looking for a place to put his Samsonite suitcase. He set the bag of bottles on the ledge by the window overlooking the building where men in brown sleeveless sweaters were now working. He opened one bottle with a practiced fingernail, steadily. The cork came out with a *pop*. He took a glass from the sideboard and poured it half full of whiskey. For a moment he stood there motionless, looking down at the building. The work, he saw without surprise, was getting done. There was glass in the window frames now; there had been none that morning. The plywood ramp had been replaced with marble steps. Abruptly he turned and called, 'Kitty! Kitty!' toward the bedroom. There was silence. 'Kitty! Kitty!' he called again. No cat appeared.

In the kitchen there was a red-legged stool by the telephone. Carrying his untasted glass of whiskey in one hand, he picked up the stool with the other and headed toward the closet at the back of the apartment. He set the whiskey on a shelf, set the stool in the closet doorway. He climbed up carefully. There was the motorcycle helmet, red, with a layer of dust on top. He pulled it down. There was something inside it. He reached in, still standing on

139

the stool, and pulled out a brown sleeveless sweater. There
were stains on the sweater. They looked like bloodstains.
He looked inside the helmet. There were stains there, too.
And there was a little blue plastic band with letters on it.
It read Paul Bendel – Paris. Once, in bed, Janet had called
him Paul. *Oh, you son of a bitch!* he said.

Getting down from the stool he thought, *For him to
know. For me to find out.* He stopped only to pick up the
drink and take it to the bathroom, where he poured it
down the toilet. Then he went into the living room and
looked out the window. The light was dimming; there
was no one on Sixty-third Street. He pushed the window
higher, leaned out. Looking to his right he could see the
intersection with Madison. He saw several of them
crossing it. One looked his way and waved. He did not
wave back. What he did was take the two bottles and drop
them down to the street where they shattered. He thought
of a man's body, shattering, in a motorcycle wreck. In
France? Certainly in France.

A group of four of them had turned the corner at
Madison and were walking toward him. All of them had
their hands in their pockets. Their heads were all inclined
together and they appeared to be having an intimate
whispered conversation. *Why whisper?* Harold thought.
can't hear you anyway.

He pulled himself up and sat on the window ledge
letting his legs hang over. He stared down at them and
forced himself to say aloud, 'Paul.' They were directly
below him now, huddled and whispering. They seemed
not to have heard him.

He took a breath and said it louder: '*Paul.*' And then he
found somewhere the strength to shout it, in a loud, clear
steady voice. 'Paul,' he shouted. '*Paul Bendel.*'

Then the four faces looked up, shocked. 'You're Paul
Bendel,' he said. 'Go back to your grave in France, Paul

They stood transfixed. Harold looked over toward
Madison. Two of them there had stopped in their tracks in
the middle of the intersection.

The four faces below were now staring up at him in

140

mute appeal, begging for his silence. His voice spoke to this appeal with strength and clarity: 'Paul Bendel,' he said, '*you must go back to France.*'

Abruptly all four of them averted their eyes from his and from one another's. Their bodies seemed to become slack. Then they began drifting apart, walking dispiritedly away from one another and from him.

He was redoing a smeared place on the painting when the telephone rang. It was Janet. She was clearly in a good mood and she asked if the zucchini soup had been all right.

'Fine,' he said. 'I had it cold.'

She laughed. 'I'm glad it wasn't too burned. How was the *jarret de veau*?'

Immediately, at the French, his stomach tightened. Despite the present clarity of his mind, he felt the familiar pain of the old petulance and jealousy. For a moment, he hugged the pain to himself, then dismissed it with a sigh.

'It's in the oven right now,' he said. 'I'm having it for dinner.'

Echo

'How many electrodes are there in that thing?' Arthu
said.

Mel gave him an irritated look. 'More than anyon
could count, old buddy.' He was checking some of th
connections of the coils that went from the big tap
recorder to the helmet; they were as profuse on the helme
as Medusa's snakes. Arthur and Mel had left the part
upstairs to come down to Mel's basement laboratory. Me
taught paraphysics at the University.

'You mean you don't *know* how many there are? Yo
put the fucker together and you don't know yourself?'

'*I* didn't put the fucker together, old buddy.' Mel gave
jerk to the coil between his hands and somewhere deep i
the recording device there was a *click*. 'A Hewlet
Packard computer did. I only told it what to make, and i
made it.'

Arthur just stared at him. Then he took an annoye
swallow from the glass of whiskey in his hand. *Thes*
Goddamn paraphysicists. It would be just like the sons c
bitches not to want to know how many connections you ha
to make to record an entire human mind. But he sai
nothing. When Denise had talked him into doing th
thing he had made enough objections. Such as, 'Why me
Why should I be the guinea pig for some crazy attempt t
make a recording of a whole personality?' Denise's answe
had merely been, 'Because Mel is your *friend*.' And so o

So he sat and drank his drink and watched Mel finis
checking out the helmet and submitted quietly when Me
placed the heavy thing on his head. He could just bare
see beneath and around dangling wires and he wa
wondering how long he would have to put up with it t
please his wife and Mel when he heard and slightly sa
Mel walk over to the recorder and heard him say, 'He

we go, old buddy.' Then he threw a switch . . .

And Arthur awoke to a world askew and furred. Something was madly wrong with his vision, even though the wires were gone. His eyes could not encapsulate the scene for him; all he really saw were pale colors, pale lights, some slight movements. There were smells somewhere, too, but they made no sense: roses, maybe, and vinegar. Somebody somewhere was singing in Chinese, or Anglo-Saxon. He closed his eyes. Only one thing was certain. He had an erection. He went to sleep.

Even the dreams were not right. They seemed to be someone else's dreams.

Days passed. He woke from time to time, and was fed. Sometimes there were tall, slim people in the room with him. They spoke Chinese. Or Anglo-Saxon. Once a long-haired person spoke to him in strange English, 'How are *you*, sir or madam?' He had no answer for that.

Finally he woke up and was able to focus his eyes and brain well enough to see that he was not in his own body. He learned that from his arms, which were hairless and chocolate. Was he a Black? A Polynesian? He did not feel as shocked as it seemed he should have felt. *Drugged? Very likely. Whom by? God knows.* He felt of his face. It was all wrong: the nose was too broad, the chin too soft, the ears were too big. *Why is it I'm not upset at this? Drugs?* But then he had been wanting to be dead for over a year, had been thinking of suicide with the intensity that some of his colleagues had when they thought of a promotion. So maybe whatever had happened to him didn't make any difference. If he didn't like it he could always kill himself. And there was no pain in whatever was going on. He felt all right.

A person in a sort of well-tailored red bathrobe came into the room. He was tall and thin and pale, and his face was smiling shyly. His hair was blond and straight and came down nearly to his waist. Or maybe it was a she. But then the person spoke and the voice was male. 'How are *you* nowadays?' The man was smiling at him more broadly

143

now.

'I'm okay,' Arthur said. 'But where am I? And who?' He held up his dark brown arm. 'In this . . . body?'

The other man looked pleased. 'It's artful,' he said.

Arthur stared at him. '*Artful?*'

The man looked embarrassed. Then he said, 'Artificial.'

'Artificial?'

'Your body,' the man said, with more confidence. 'It i artificial now.'

'For Christ's sake,' Arthur said. And then, 'I liked th other one well enough.'

The man smiled sweetly. 'Long dead,' he said. 'An rotten.'

'Jesus Christ,' Arthur said. 'Jesus Christ.'

He slept after that and the next day the long-haired ma was there when he awoke. Arthur assumed that a day ha passed because the man's bathrobe was yellow this time Arthur had a question ready. 'Where did this body com from?'

The man smiled at him with encouragement. 'Cleveland'

He hadn't been ready for that. He felt he might never b ready for whatever this childlike and epicene person migh tell him. 'Did you grow this body in Cleveland, c something?'

'Or something is correct. We made you first i Cleveland in bodily form before we grew you big in here The mind was poured into you. Poured into your prett and always body.' The man looked at him quizzicall: 'Bodies not made in Cleveland in your time?'

'In my time?'

'In your time of the world. When you was alive and we and running around.'

Arthur continued to stare. 'Is this the *future*?' he sai

The man shook his head. 'It's only nowadays,' he sai 'Like always.' Then he smiled. 'And you was born in th twenty-second century anno domini, in crowded tim and places?'

Arthur let out a heavy sigh. Then he said, 'Can you g

me a drink? With whiskey or gin? Ethyl alcohol?'

The man did not seem to understand.

'An intoxicating drink.'

The man smiled again. 'I understand that thing. And yes, I will.' He turned to leave the room. 'Not the twenty-second century anno domini?'

'The twentieth,' Arthur said in a voice near a whisper. Finally it was all coming down on him. 'What century is this?'

The man turned and smiled at him before he left the room. 'The forty-seventh,' he said. 'Anno domini.'

The drink turned out to be a sort of screwdriver – spiked orange juice. It was in a simple glass that did not look at all futuristic. After Arthur drank it, he said, 'How did I get here? In this body from . . . from Cleveland?'

'Refrigerator,' the man said. 'We found a refrigerator, all wrapped and sealed underground where a city was. With a tape of you inside. Under rubble. From time so far and distant long agone so hard to tell.'

From time so far and distant long agone . . .' Have you a name?' Arthur asked.

'Yes. I am always Ben.'

'Ben?'

'Yes. Always Ben.'

Arthur began to sit up for the first time. It was not as difficult as he had feared it might be. He felt fairly strong. 'What kind of tape, Ben?'

'Oh, machine tape. Ancient computer tape,' Ben said. 'They had all of you all over on the tape. Except a body.'

Arthur had already figured that one out. Some time or other, even years after that night with the thing on his head, Mel had stuck that tape in a refrigerator for some reason. And twenty-seven centuries later somebody had dug it out, freakishly preserved, and figured out what it was: a record of the memory, mind, imagination, personality, lusts, ambitions, neuroses and everything else of Arthur Franks. Then somebody had gotten some kind of artificial body from a factory in Cleveland and had played the tape into it. And here he was, reconstructed from some point before his life's end. Somewhere out in this strange world the dust of his first life lay; he was now being given a chance to live out the last part of that life again. If he wanted to.

How long had he lived, a near-suicide, back in the twentieth century? Had he killed himself?

'You found me as a recording,' he said. 'Without a body.'

'Yes,' Ben said. 'And as a student of the ancient tongue of English and of old times long agone I had you made especially a body. To have a thing to put the tape into so then to talk with me. As we indeed are doing now.'

'Do you know anything more about me? Like when I . . . died? Or about my wife?'

Ben looked sad, his normally smooth forehead wrinkling. 'Sorry always.' Then he smiled. 'All I know for sure and always is America was home for you.'

'Okay,' Arthur said. Maybe it was better not to know what had become of himself – of that other himself. 'Is there still an America?'

Ben continued smiling. 'Two. One north and one is always south.'

'That's good to know,' Arthur said. 'Could I have another drink?'

The bathroom was much like a twentieth-century one except that the water from the taps was scented and the light coming from the ceiling was like daylight – yellowish and very pleasant to his eyes. Over the sink was a mirror

He stood and stared at himself for several minutes shocked.

He was very Negroid and very handsome, with a short Afro of glossy black hair, a broad nose, generous ears thick lips and clear eyes. His shoulders were broad and the chest beneath them was smooth, hairless, and powerful His stomach was flat, his arms well muscled but soft looking, like a woman's.

He stood back to see himself full length. His body wa

146

perfect; there wasn't a blemish on it. He looked at his face again – his new face – and smiled. *What the hell,* he thought, *this beats suicide.*

Later, when Arthur was able to walk a little each day, Ben brought others. Some were apparently women – very calm, straightforward types, like Ben. But none of them spoke English. They smiled a lot. They were all nice-looking, but a bit forceless, passive; and they all seemed young. He wondered if they had some way of staying young-looking whatever their ages. Probably so. Or maybe their bodies came from another factory in Cleveland.

He liked the sounds of the women's voices, more like Chinese than Anglo-Saxon, soft and slurred in speech and with musical pitch. Sometimes they sang. He liked the way they moved around and looked over at him, in his bed, from time to time, with curiosity but with no hint of flirtatiousness.

Outside the room's only window, where the view was of an empty field and, beyond that, a dark row of trees, it was raining heavily under an iron-colored sky. There was no work of human building to be seen from that window, only grass and sky and the line of trees.

Ben left the room for a while and returned with another woman, different from the others, and stood with her near the door and talked for a moment. Arthur looked at her. She was dressed like the others in some kind of a tan robe. But her hair was cut short and her face had a puzzled animation about it and a sense of some quality – urgency maybe – that was missing in the others. She had very pale skin and auburn hair; she was tall and her figure was splendid.

Ben brought her over and introduced her to him as Annabel. Surprisingly, she spoke English. He was astonished at this at first, until she smiled and said, 'Ben tells me I'm from the same century you're from. We thought it was the twenty-second at first.'

'Don't you remember?' Arthur said.

'No,' she said, 'I don't remember. Something about the way the tapes were played into this body, Ben says. I know how to speak, but I don't remember a thing . . .' She looked toward Ben.

'It is always amnesia,' Ben said. 'She was the first to be made from ancient tapes a year ago. But the tapes were not right for her brain so she forgot it all. She forgot all the time long agone when she lived before. Then we made you and did always better with your tape.'

'Maybe it's best not to remember,' Arthur said.

She smiled at him wistfully. 'Still I'd like to know. I don't even know what my name was. I'd like you to tell me about our time – the twentieth century – and maybe it'll help me remember.'

'Sure,' Arthur said. 'What do you want to know?'

For several weeks she came to his room at breakfast and asked questions. He told her about cities and government and clothing and animals and the way things looked and how people lived. But none of it touched her memory. Arthur liked her, and there seemed at times something familiar about her. It made sense that there would be since she had probably been taped by Mel – possibly after the same dinner party, after he himself had been 'copied' onto the tapes. She could be Denise. Except she wasn't and he knew that. Maybe she was the wife of someone he knew, some woman he had talked to briefly once and then forgot about. She was clearly as intelligent as he, and a quick; her vocabulary was excellent. And her personality – something about her personality sometimes haunted him. He would be drinking coffee with her and would happen to look at her hand holding the cup or at the way she brought the cup to her lips and there would be something terrible familiar about it. But he could no place it. It was like *déjà vu*.

On his first day outside, with Ben gently helping him wal on wobbly legs, the thing he felt most was the clarity an cleanness of the outside air. It was a spring morning, wit

148

small leaves on the trees by the door of the building; on the grass near the door a thick robin stood attentive, its ear cocked toward the ground. A small white dog scampered as such dogs always had toward a hill and then disappeared from view. There was a warm breeze, riffling his kinky hair.

Arthur walked a few yards, then turned to look at the building he had just left for the first time. It seemed to be made of green stone, with a slightly peaked green roof, and large windows. Except for the green color it could have been a large bank from downtown St Louis or Denver. There were five other buildings, more or less like it, making a complex, with gray rubbery walkways between them. At a distance two long-haired men walked hand in hand in quiet conversation from one building to another, one of them smoking a cigarette. Arthur's heart was light, his stomach fluttery with the warmth of the day and the sense of the new. They walked around the building and Arthur stood and looked toward the dark green line of woods in the distance and then they went back inside; he was still too weak to walk anymore. But he could tell that the body he inhabited was healthy and youthful and would soon be strong. There were firm muscles under the brown skin; his arms and legs were straight, well formed; and there were good, springy arches in his feet. His hands were capacious and wise; he could sense the power, the aptitude and heft, of them.

The next day he and Annabel went for a walk, going about a third of the way down the gray path toward the woods before he became too tired to go further.

They said little. For a few moments he took her hand, but he sensed something in her that stiffened when he did so. Somehow, he felt no desire for her, even though she was clearly a lovely woman, and he could not understand why. There was nothing wrong with his sexuality in this new and young body; even in his old, haggard and soft one there had been no problems there. He had always been a strong lover; that alone had kept him going for years against the tide of his old life that had pulled so strongly in other ways toward death. Toward drink, and guilt, and alienation and despair.

But Annabel with her fine breasts and firm round ass did not turn him on. He could not understand it.

Later, in his room, when she was in a chrome-and-leather chair and he was lying against the pillows in bed, he tried talking about it. 'If this were a movie,' he said, 'we would be falling in love by now.'

She looked toward him thoughtfully. 'I suppose so. I think I may be homosexual. A lesbian.'

He looked at her. What she said seemed true. Maybe that explained his lack of feeling toward her. 'Do you find the women here attractive?'

'No,' she said, and then smiled at him. 'I bet you don't either.'

He smiled back. 'No, I don't,' he said. And then, 'Why don't you come over here and kiss me on the mouth? It couldn't hurt anything.'

'Okay,' she said and got up. She walked over toward him, seated herself on the edge of the bed, bent over slowly, and kissed him, with her mouth open and soft. At first he felt almost nothing, as though he were kissing the smooth palm of his own hand. But they held the kiss and, gradually, he felt an excitement begin in his stomach. It was a different feeling from what he was used to; there was some kind of very strong and frightening power to it. He continued kissing her, working his lips a bit now but not using his tongue and not reaching his hands toward her breasts that hung down over his chest. There *was* some great power there; but something in him would not let him yield to it. There was something he was afraid of. He pulled away from her, and looked up. Her face was very serious and just a bit frightened.

'Something is scaring me,' he said quietly.

'Me too,' she said. 'I think I'd better go.'

She got up from the bed and left the room without saying good-bye. He lay there silently for a long while thinking of her. Somewhere in his stomach there was still a ribbon of unpleasantness – of fear. But the fear was being buried by the excitement of desire, becoming indistinguishable from it.

In the middle of that night he was awakened by her wet mouth kissing his breasts, under the sheet. He could smell the faint smell of sweat from her warm body – had been smelling it even while asleep. It aroused him immediately. Then without saying a word she moved her head down to him and took him in her mouth. Still in his stomach was the ribbon of fear, but the excitement, the movement toward ecstasy, buried it. And he exploded into her mouth, beneath the sheet. She stayed with him, holding his hips, for only a minute afterward and then left, padding slowly – somehow, it seemed, thoughtfully – out of the room in bare feet, leaving him alone in bed. Neither of them had said a word.

He did not see her the next morning at breakfast; for several days she had been joining him for the farrago of oats and wheat and honey that a silent male nurse brought him every morning together with a yellow cup full of powerful, astringent coffee. Nor did she join him for his lunch of odd-looking vegetables and what he thought of as 'Mystery Soup.'

Ben dropped in on him after lunch for a conversation about twentieth-century America; Arthur told him about movies and cars. His heart wasn't in it; he could not get Annabel off his mind.

'Are there still cars?' he asked Ben.

'Oh, no. Very little mechanical nowadays.'

'How do you travel?'

'Walking. Always walking,' Ben said. 'Sometimes we use a flyer, for traveling long.'

'Is a flyer an airplane?'

'Somewhat,' Ben said. 'But no motor and no jets.'

'How does it work?'

'Nobody knows,' Ben said. 'No need to know.'

'Who does the cooking around here?'

'Cooking?' Ben said.

'Yes. Preparing food to eat.' He almost said 'always'

151

before 'eat.'

'Food is always assembled,' Ben said. 'Assembled from little atoms by the cooker. Like clothes and buildings.'

'Oh,' Arthur said, and thought *Jesus.* 'Then nobody does any work?'

'I study things. Always ancient America. Others study things. And we talk a lot.'

'And that's all you do?'

Ben smiled at him benignly. 'Always.'

'I've never seen any children around, Ben. Do you have children in other places?'

'No. No children. And there are only very few and small other places and no children there. Only big ones like you and me.'

'Then what . . . ? Then how do you reproduce?'

Ben smiled and shook his head. 'Oh, we never reproduce. We always live ourselves. Always.'

'You're *immortal*?'

'Oh, of course,' Ben said. 'We live forever. And you indeed will live forever too in that strong body.'

'*Jesus*,' he said aloud and lay back against the pillows. And then, 'Don't you get *bored*?'

'Oh, sure,' Ben said. 'But it goes away. And we forget a lot and always learn things over.'

'How old are you, Ben?'

Ben shook his head. 'I never know at all how old. Centuries. Someday I'll die myself by fire as others do and that will be an end.'

'Then someday you'll tire of it and kill yourself. And that's been happening for some time now and there aren't many left.'

Ben smiled dolefully, his youthful and bland face registering a kind of pleasant painfulness. 'That's all there is to know,' he said.

Ben turned to leave, walking out of the room with his loose-jointed gait, his long hair covering his narrow shoulders and back. At the door he stopped and turned back toward Arthur. 'Long life is good enough for most,' he said, 'and death is not so bad.'

Arthur said nothing. When Ben was gone he began working at the room's little table on the chess set he was making from a soft material like Styrofoam. He was using a knife that Ben had gotten him, and he began working on the most difficult pieces, the knights, carving them with a great deal of care.

When he had finished the first one and had begun to copy it for the second, Annabel came in. She was wearing a green robe and she looked beautiful to him.

At first he did not know what to say. Then he looked at her and said, 'Thanks. Thanks for last night.'

'Sure,' she said. 'It was strange. But I liked it.'

'Then you aren't a lesbian,' he said, trying to make his voice light but feeling some kind of embarrassment in it. He set the unfinished piece and the knife on the desk in front of him and swiveled in the chair to see her better. She was tall and fair-skinned – a beautiful woman. 'Would you like to take a walk?' he said. 'I think I could make it to the woods.'

She was silent for a minute. Then she said, 'Sure.' She walked over to the table and carefully, thoughtfully, picked up the finished piece and held it between thumb and forefinger. 'This is a knight,' she said.

He stared at her. 'How did you know that?' Chess did not exist, as far as he had been able to find out, in this world. Ben's people did not play games. 'It's a twentieth-century thing.'

'I don't know,' she said. 'I really don't. I just know it's called a knight.'

'Do you know what "chess" means?' he said.

'"Chess"?' She said the word carefully. 'No. No, I don't.'

He shook his head and then took the piece from her and set it down by the finished pawns. 'Let's take that walk.'

While they were walking and he had his hands in the pockets of his robe and his eyes down on the strange plastic shoes he had been given, he said, 'Ben tells me I'll be very strong when my body has a chance to . . . to ripen or whatever it is.'

'Do you look the way you looked before? In your other life?' she said.

'No,' he said. 'God, no. I was white, and middle-aged. A professor of chemistry and getting pot-bellied.'

'Yes,' she said. 'I have no idea what I looked like, but I know it wasn't like this.' She extended her long and pale arms from her sides, palms upward, and looked earnestly at him. 'I know I'm entirely different now from what I once was.'

'It's a strange feeling,' he said. 'Still, the way you look now is fine by me.' But that wasn't exactly true; there was a touch of idle and self-assuring flattery in it. She was beautiful enough, but he still was not at ease with her beauty. Something about it haunted him as though at times there were superimposed upon her face and body another face and body, from his past, very faint but disquieting.

He did make it to the woods, although he was tired when he got there. Ben had told him it would take months to get the full strength of his new body. The body had been cloned from synthetic, composite genes, but it had never been exercised and its muscles were soft and new.

In the woods they sat on a fallen log and smoked the odd-tasting cigarettes that Ben supplied them with. Then they began to make love, slowly and cautiously, first with their hands and then with their mouths. He brought her to a light orgasm in the spotted daylight that filtered through old trees, while she sat on the log dreamily and he kneeled in front of her. After that they found a grassy clearing with dry ground and lay together. Somehow they were perfectly matched, and knew exactly what to do for each other.

But then, as he was beginning to feel the oncoming orgasm, she looked down on him from her position above him and said, 'Jesus, do I love this.' The words fell somehow like lead on his spirit and he became suddenly afraid, frozen in his movements. The same fear came in her face. They stared at each other while his soul shrank from her. He did not know what had happened; he only knew that her words – words that were somehow terribly familiar to him – had frightened him. Forest light flecked her beautiful and glowing skin; her fine breasts were warm in his upward-reaching hands; somewhere a bird was singing jubilantly, and wind rustled the leaves of the trees. Inside himself he was cold, trembling. He rolled out from under her and lay on the grass in turmoil – frightened and angry. 'What happened?' he said.

'I don't know. I said that, and something went wrong. I don't know.'

He shook his head. 'Maybe it's these new bodies,' he said. 'Maybe we'll have to just get used to them.'

She shook her head and said nothing.

He did not see her for several days and was relieved not to. He spent the time easily enough – when he was not troubled by thinking about her – finishing his chess set, exercising lightly, and wandering through the building where he lived.

On the third day Ben and another man whose only English was the word 'Hello' took him to the far end of the building to a laboratory. There were four large tanks, coffin-like and bright green, lined up along one wall. Ben walked over to the second of these from the left, set his long-fingered hand on its lid, and said, 'This is where we grew your self for years.'

Arthur walked over to it and Ben lifted the hinged lid for him. Inside it was like a large, green bathtub, with about half a dozen little metal pipes entering it on one side. 'How long was I in this thing?' he asked.

'Three years,' Ben said. 'No way to go faster.'

'Was it difficult to play the tape into . . . into me?'

Ben smiled and shook his head. 'Oh, yes,' he said. 'We did it wrong two times. First we had the body wrong and next the tape. But then we got you always right and here you stand.' Then he looked at the other man with him, who was apparently some kind of technician, and the other nodded toward Ben with a faint smile.

Arthur started to pursue this but Ben, abruptly for him, turned and walked over to one of the consoles and took from an otherwise empty shelf a box about the size of a candy box, walked back to Arthur and handed it to him. 'Here is your soul,' he said, softly.

Arthur took the box in both hands. 'My tape?' he said.

'Of course,' Ben said. 'Your ancient tape. Your soul.'

Arthur opened the box with care. Inside was a full plastic reel with a label that read 'Advent Corporation Boston, Mass.' And under that someone had written with a ballpoint pen, 'Arthur Franks.'

That evening he finished his chess set and then made a board by ruling the sixty-four squares on a sheet of white flexible plastic and darkening half of them with what seemed to be a Magic Marker. It was late and he was tired but he set the pieces up, the white ones on his side of the board, and began to play King's Gambit against the black, using Morphy's way of sacrificing the king's knight for a heavy attack on black's kingside. It was strange to see his brown arm and hand moving chess pieces around on a board; he thought he had become used to his new color – even liked it – but it was a shock to see himself in this old context; he had been captain of his chess club in high school and when other kids had been out shooting basketball or stealing hubcaps or whatever, he had sat in his room at home working out variations of chess attacks. But with a thin white arm, a pale hand on the pieces – not this smooth and chocolate arm with the big and nimble hand at the end of it.

Outside the window was a nearly full moon in a jet black sky. The window was open, and warm air, hinting of summer nights, filled the room. He could hear the shrill sounds of tree frogs and somewhere a cricket.

Then the door opened quietly and Annabel walked in. He turned to look at her. She was barefoot, dressed in white robe. Her hair had been pulled back and was tied

156

behind her head, framing her face. She was lovely. He felt tense, frightened. 'What do you want?' he said.

'I wanted to make love the way I did before. I thought you would be asleep.' Each word came to him as if it had been spoken for him before, as if he had thought it just before she said it. *Déjà vu*. He shook his head, trying to shake it off.

'No,' he said. 'I don't want that right now.'

'I know,' she said. She took off her robe and sat on the edge of the bed. 'I think we ought to start where we left off yesterday.'

He stared at her as she lay back, naked, against a pillow. 'I don't know if I can . . .'

'Yes, you can,' she said. 'That was only a barrier for us. We've crossed it now.'

'I was thinking something like that myself,' he said. He came over and sat beside her on the bed.

'Sure you were,' she said. 'We're really very much alike. We think the same things.'

He slipped off his sandals. 'You're really something,' he said.

'So are you,' she said.

She was right. The barrier or whatever it was had fallen. The fear had subsided. The pleasure of lovemaking was different from what it had been before for him, with other women he had had. It was very inward, very intense. He hardly looked at her.

When he climaxed something seemed to open up inside him. There was a sense of release in a secret part of himself, at the center of his aching and suicidal life. His eyes were shut and he heard himself laughing, immersing himself in himself.

He lay back afterward, spent and blissful. They did not speak, nor did they look at one another. He stared at the moon outside the window, the early summer moon, as old and luminous and clear in the black sky as was his soul within himself.

They slept together that night for the first time. Not touching, but naked together in the same bed, each turned to the right in a nearly fetal position, like a pair of twins.

In the morning they awoke silently together and silently drank coffee, sitting side by side in bed. There seemed to be no need to speak.

And then, as they were drinking their second cup of coffee, she began looking at something on the other side of him and he saw that it was the chessboard, still set up from the night before. She was looking at it intently and her eyes began to widen.

'What is it?' he said. 'Is something wrong?'

'That's the King's Gambit,' she said. 'Morphy's Attack.'

Something prickled at the back of his neck and he heard a tremor in his own voice. '*Yes, it is*,' he said.

'And the next move is bishop takes bishop's pawn.' She turned and stared at him, her eyes wide and her lips trembling.

'Yes,' he said. 'Bishop takes bishop's pawn . . . Not many people know that.'

'I've known it since high school,' she said. 'Grover Cleveland High School. Where I was . . .'

'Captain of the chess team.' His voice was like gravel in his throat. His heart was pounding and his mouth was dry. 'Ben's mistake,' he said, whispering because his dry mouth made him whisper it. 'You're Ben's wrong body.'

And she whispered too. 'I'm Arthur Franks,' she said.

'Oh Jesus,' he said. 'Oh sweet Jesus.' He lay back in bed and stared at the ceiling for a long while. And then, later, when a calmness had come into him and he let his hand reach out slowly and gently and let it fall sensuously upon her smooth and cool thigh he felt, at exactly the same instant, her hand soft and sexual upon his own thigh. 'Oh yes,' he said aloud, softly. 'Oh, yes.'

And he heard her say it too. 'Oh, yes. Oh, yes.'

Sitting in Limbo

Sitting here in Limbo, I have found I can return to and make corrections in the life I once lived. I calculate that seventeen years have passed since I died in Columbus, Ohio; it was about two years ago that I learned to return to various parts of my life and change them for the better. The work is difficult but rewarding. And what else has a dead person to do with his time?

There are no physical discomforts here under this pale and sunless sky; the boredom and emptiness that make up my existence are not intolerable. In many ways it is not as bad as being alive was. There is no one to talk to here and nothing, really, to think about except that life of fifty-one years that I was permitted to have. From my present perspective I see it as a unity, like a complex circuit diagram or an abstract-expressionist painting. I see that a part here or there may be altered – a diode or a blob of color – and the pattern will be forever changed. From my birth in the Good Samaritan Hospital in Lexington, Kentucky, to my death from a coronary in Columbus, it is all a single, sometimes baffling, entity. And I can change it now, a small part at a time. I have the distance.

It was quite by accident that I discovered I could go back there. I have seven chairs here on which I can sit; they have been here since I arrived. Each is different from the others. One of them is a hard wooden chair of varnished oak. I sit in it when I wish to be wakeful. Sometimes I let myself drowse in a reverie for days; at other times I sit upright, my body expectant, waiting. There is, of course, nothing to wait *for* here, but I take comfort in adopting the posture. The wooden chair is exactly right for this. It is high-backed and sturdy; it squeaks when I shift my weight from one buttock to the other. There are very few noises here in Limbo and I appreciate the contribution this chair makes.

I was sitting in it some time ago when I became reminded of a desk at Morton Junior High School, in Lexington. It, too, was made of varnished oak and it, too, squeaked. It had an arm on it for writing and my Limbo chair does not, but otherwise they are much alike. I was sitting in the chair and staring at the fuzzy horizon of Limbo and squeaking every minute or so in a kind of slow dirge. And suddenly my memory came alive with myself in the eighth grade, in Miss Ralston's Social Science class. That class met for an hour every day after lunch, and it was one of the most tedious things in my life. Remembering it here was like *déjà vu*; perhaps I had been in a kind of Limbo then and had not known it. I remembered the gravelly sound of Miss Ralston's voice. I remembered the way she would adjust her teeth in her mouth with a kind of sucking between paragraphs. I remembered her dark flowered dresses, her grayish hair in a bun, her heavy brown shoes. I remembered the fight to stay awake.

And then I remembered a whimsical promise I had made myself as a teen-aged boy in that classroom: I promised I would return to that room at that time if I ever learned the secret of time travel when I grew up. I imagined myself astonishing everyone by my sudden appearance. I would be a grown and vigorous time traveler stepping with confidence from a glass-and-chromium machine that would materialize just to the right of Miss Ralston's desk. She would stop in midsentence and her jaw would drop. Everyone would stare. In that fantasy I was both observer and observed, both adult and boy, and the imagined pleasure was exquisite.

Then, in Limbo, I remembered the date I had made myself that promise: September 23, 1942. I was born in 1928, so I must have been fourteen. I had repeated the date over and over in that classroom so I would remember it years later. And clearly it had worked. I was joyful, pleased with the continuity.

Then something inside me told me to cross my ankles in a certain way and to slump in my oak chair in a certain way and to breathe in slowly and I did all this without really thinking about it and there I was. I was in Miss Ralston's classroom in September of 1942. But I did not materialize as a grown man to see myself sitting as a young student. I found myself as that student again – ankles crossed, slumped in my chair, breathing in slowly. I heard Miss Ralston's voice droning about the primary exports of Latin America. Fawn Harrington was on my left in a green tartan skirt and green sweater; Toby Kavanaugh sat on my right. I was wearing my Thom McAn shoes, the brown ones. They were too tight and my feet hurt. I had a headache; Mother and Daddy had been fighting in the kitchen the night before and I barely slept. I hadn't done my homework. Fawn had tried flirting with me before class but I had ignored her. I did not like flirts; I always felt they were up to something.

It was all completely familiar and all clear and real. It was no dream. I tried to stand, to get up and leave that awful room; but I could not. I found that I had no control over my body. It was doing whatever it had done on that day the first time I had lived it. I was only there, it seemed, as an observer. I felt that I could return to Limbo whenever I willed it. I calmed myself and watched.

Miss Ralston finished her reading and then called on Jack Mowbray to read. He stood – a sly, freckled boy whom I distrusted – and read a paragraph about Simon Bolivar. Miss Ralston corrected his pronunciation of Bolivar, pronouncing it poorly herself. She called on Marylinne Saunders to read. And on it went. I watched and listened, fascinated, waiting for it to come to me. I had no awareness of what I was thinking – that other, fourteen-year-old I – but I began to be aware that this was a time when something bad had happened. It was about to happen again. It was going to happen when I was called on to read. I sat in the second row; it would be soon.

When it came to me I found myself standing up awkwardly and looking down at the text. I knew that a

161

humiliation was coming but I could not remember what it was. I heard myself begin to read. My voice was tired and a bit resentful.

Suddenly I was shocked by Miss Ralston's voice, harshly interrupting me. 'Billy!' she said. 'Billy Whaley. Will you please consider your appearance?'

I looked at her stupidly.

She stared at me with an ironic, prissy frown. 'Please go to the boy's room and button yourself.' There was something triumphantly cruel in her voice, and it withered me. I looked down. My corduroys were open at the fly, unbuttoned. I heard a snicker from somewhere behind me, the snicker of a female voice . . .

Immediately I was back in Limbo. I was alone, standing in front of my oak chair, looking down. I am always in faded jeans here. They never wear out, never become dirty. Their fly was properly zipped, as always. I sighed aloud with relief and sat down. I was still shaking. I felt, in some obscure way, a victim.

There is a progression of time here. There are nights and days even though there is no visible sun, and I count them and remember the count. That is how I know it is seventeen years since I died. I do not know if I will be here for eternity or not. There has been no judgment of me, no communication from any god, devil or angel. Nothing has been promised, nothing explained, and I do not care. Yet I have come to believe that there may be a way out of Limbo. I have begun to feel that if I properly edit and rectify my former life that I will be able to pass on from here and be reborn. I sense that I await reincarnation and another life. I feel hopeful. Change is frightening to me and yet I feel hopeful of change.

After my first experience of return I marked off ten days while I thought of various things in my former life, as I often do, or merely counted numbers in my mind as I also often do here, and then I decided to try going back to Miss Ralston's class on that same day. It would be interesting to find myself alive again, even in that dream classroom, and to be among people again. Yet I am not really bored with being dead. I could stay in Limbo for eternity. There is no pain here, no fatigue; there are no appetites. There is no danger. There are no misunderstandings.

I seated myself in the wooden chair and thought of the classroom. I visualized Miss Ralston and her false teeth and the blackboard behind her that was gray with chalk dust. I found myself crossing my ankles again and there I was again at precisely the moment I had reentered the first time. Miss Ralston was reading the same things about Latin America. She called on Jack Mowbray to read, corrected his pronunciation of Bolivar. Knowing now what was going to happen to me and knowing, too, how trivial it really was, I felt calmer this time. I decided to try something. I tried to move my hand down to my lap and button my fly. Nothing happened. My hand remained gently resting on my desk. Jack went on reading. I concentrated on moving the hand. It moved about an inch and then lay still again. Jack finished reading and Miss Ralston called on Fawn Harrington to read. Fawn stood up – a beautiful, soft-voiced girl with long lashes – and read quietly. Concentrating, I made my mind picture my right hand lifting from the desk and settling into my lap and after a moment I realized with surprise that it now *was* in my lap. I began picturing my fingers fastening the buttons. It was slow and difficult, but I could feel it happening. I got them buttoned.

When the reading came to me I stood up and read a passage about the principal fuels of Latin America and then sat down. Miss Ralston had not spoken to me! She called on Toby Kavanaugh. Toby stood up, his open book close to his weak eyes, and began to read. And then I found myself back here in Limbo, sitting in my wooden chair. I was exultant, almost awed. I had changed the past!

Immediately I wondered if that change would provoke others further along. Would I be less shy and difficult with girls when I began to date them at seventeen? Would I make a better grade in Social Science, do better in college, get a better job when I graduated, and so on? Such changes might well prevent my death at fifty-one. Yet clearly I was still dead and nothing in Limbo had changed. It was the same as ever, such as it was.

I remembered my first job interview, in my twenties, when I had become frightened and couldn't even remember my telephone number when the interviewer asked for it. Would erasing the incident of the unbuttoned fly have made me more confident in my twenties? I had invented a phone number for that man and he had ended the interview later, saying, 'I'll call you.'

I had sat in an armchair in that office, somewhat like the one I have in Limbo. I got up from the oak chair and seated myself in the armchair. I gripped its arms with my hands as I remembered doing. My body fell into that old tense position as though I were an actor who had played the scene a thousand times.

And there I was living it again in a small room with Currier and Ives prints on the wall and the interviewer, a florid man in a brown suit, smiling blandly at me. I knew instantly that it was all as it had been and that it would not end differently. Buttoning my fly in the classroom had changed nothing.

I remained through the inventing of the phone number and then I returned to Limbo. It was clear that I could only change things one at a time; I could not start new chains of circumstance.

Eventually I was to find out that my intuition was correct. I could change particular scenes in my life, erasing mistakes as it were and adding corrections, but I could not seriously change the substantive details. I was a high school teacher for my adult life and I could not change that. I was married twice and divorced twice; I could not alter that either, although I could edit my more unfortunate scenes with my wives. Honesty compels me to say there were many of these scenes. By judicious editing over a period of Limbo-years and hundreds of trips back I was able to improve my behavior in arguments, make

164

myself kinder and more understanding, and the like. But I still divorced them and I could not change that. And truly I did not want to.

I could only make the transition to the past while sitting in the appropriate chair. I found that with some effort it was always possible to associate a chair with every part of my past I wished to explore and then, when needed, change. I have come to believe that the chairs were put here as vehicles for me to render my former life less painful to remember – less embarrassing and wrong. Perhaps other inhabitants of Limbo have more or fewer chairs. Perhaps not. I have never seen another inhabitant.

My first wife was Jane; I was married to her five years. It took me all of two years in Limbo to edit the relationship, yet with all the changes the divorce took place on the same date it had the first time around.

After three years of marriage to Jane I had lost interest in her and had stopped having sex with her. I had found – and I shudder to mention this – ways to blame her for my lack of interest. I told her that her clothes were all wrong – especially her underwear. I told her her education was lacking, that I felt she was afraid of sex. I had married her in the first place because she was a kind of boyish, no-nonsense woman, and now I blamed her for being that way, told her I wanted her to be more feminine. I told Jane in anger that I thought she was a repressed lesbian because of the way she wore blue jeans all the time. It was horrible of me to say such things. I had winced over them more than once, here in Limbo, before I discovered that I could change them. I am not a cruel person; I really wanted to erase those cruelties.

And I did. I went through the five years with Jane, making myself into a pleasant and honest person. I told her of the tapering off of my desire for her. I was kind to her in every way. She was understanding, and grateful for my straightforwardness. There were no fights.

I did not have sex with her any more than I had had originally. Living in Limbo all these years had obliterated any interest in sex for me. I made no changes in that department.

My second wife was named Millie. She was a librarian for a chemical company and very serious. Millie was a *very* serious person. It was eventually that seriousness that I learned to hate. Whenever I spoke to her even about unimportant matters like the grade of hamburger we were using or the best kinds of plant food, she was always incredibly attentive. Millie had a good figure and an earnest sexual style, but she wore drab clothes. She looked like the librarian she was to the core.

Within a year of our marriage I had stopped making love with her. I was drinking a good deal by then and I would sometimes find a seductive woman at one of the bars I went to and take her to a motel for the night. Millie would look even more serious the next day but she would never ask where I had been. I knew she felt lucky to have gotten me in the first place. I was a respected biology teacher at a large high school and my salary was far above the average. I had clean habits and was generally polite. My indiscretions were always careful. I had no interest in provoking scandal. Besides I had no real liking for any of the women I took to bed in motels. It was just something I did. Sometimes, in fact, there would be no real sex involved. I would just watch the woman undress herself, feel satisfied enough, and fall drunkenly asleep.

Yet I felt guilty. And from Limbo I was greatly relieved to make the necessary changes, to spend those motel nights at home with Millie, reading or watching television.

In something like four and a half years of Limbo-time I have managed to edit my relationships with my wives in such a way that I now feel guiltless and at ease about what happened. I have altered some other aspects of my life – as a student, a teacher and a church member. I am satisfied. I hope to be reborn, to have another life. So far it has not happened, but it may not take place immediately. Limbo is slow, and I understand that. I would like to be reborn as a woman – as a vivacious and sexy woman. Why not?

Days pass and nothing happens. I sit and wait, moving

from chair to chair. Must I go back and reedit? Was I wrong in expecting a second life after rectifying the first? I think not. I feel certain that good editing will propel me toward a new existence. I no longer feel content with Limbo. I am ready to move on. I want to be a girl. I want my name to be Beth. I want to be white, middle-class, pretty, and I want to be given a good education and be well dressed.

One of my chairs is smaller than the others. It is clear to me now that it is a child's chair. I have never sat on it. I am beginning to feel that I must, however uncomfortable it may be, if I am to finish my first life properly. I must sit in the child's chair. I am afraid to.

Eventually I sat in the small chair. I folded my hands in my lap, because that seemed the thing to do, and inclined my head. The chair was not uncomfortable at all. I felt quite natural and comfortable in it. I closed my eyes.

When I opened them after a bit I found that I was looking at my own small knees. They were bare below short pants and were scraped and rough-looking the way boys' knees sometimes are. I looked up. I was sitting facing the corner of a small bedroom papered in pink wallpaper. To my right was an open closet and to my left a bed. It was Mother's bedroom. I had been sent there to sit in the corner for an hour because of something bad I had done. I was not to speak or squirm or wriggle. I felt terribly uncomfortable and for a moment I panicked and almost willed myself back here to Limbo, but I decided to hold off for a while to see that would happen. My heart was beating fast. I was about six years old and I knew I had been here in this chair in the corner many times and I knew that something important was going to take place. Something would happen that always happened when I was sent to sit in the corner. I began to have a dim sense that I had *wanted* to be sent there, had done something deliberately bad so that it would happen.

Time passed. I sat and tried to remember how my mother had looked when I was a small child, but I could not. My father – that weak, almost absent man – had told me that she was an 'extraordinarily beautiful' woman when he had married her. All I could remember was the way she had looked in the few years before she had died, when I was in my late thirties. Both of my wives had hated her and said I was too good to her, had resented the closeness of the two of us. Well. That had been their problem, not mine. I only saw my mother when she came to visit. She was thick-waisted and had gray hair then and she wore cheap print dresses. But she was fun to talk to and she laughed a lot when we would sit and drink sherry together in the living room. Mother could be really funny when she was a little tipsy, and she was devastating in the way she could point out the pretensions of others. I have always admired her mind.

I sat there for about twenty minutes and thought of Mother and her false teeth and her wit and the big gestures she would use when talking and how she would say things like 'to my utter astonishment' and 'That, my dear, will be the day.' Whatever my wives had said, she was a pleasure to be with.

And then in my chair there in the past I heard footsteps behind me and heard a voice saying, 'Billy, it's getting too warm in the living room. I'm going to change into something cooler. You mustn't look.'

She had stopped talking before I recognized with a distinct shock that it had been Mother's voice. It was the same cadence that I had remembered, but so much more youthful, so much ... so much *richer*, than when I was grown up. I heard more footsteps. I heard her opening a drawer somewhere in back of me.

On the inside of the closet door to my right was a full-length, framed mirror. The frame was enameled in a creamy yellowish-white. A few men's jackets hung in the closet – gray and brown ones – and I knew they were Daddy's and that Daddy was away. Daddy was almost always away. Somehow I was glad he was.

I could see the mirror without moving my head. All I had to do was open my eyes slightly and look to the right.

The mirror reflected the bed and part of a white-painted dresser, with silver-backed brushes on it and two photographs. One photograph was of me as a baby, the other was of Mother herself; they were both in yellowed ivory frames.

And then someone came into view in the mirror and something deep in me thrilled to see. It was Mother; I could tell even though her back was toward the mirror because she was walking toward the bed. Her waist was slim and her step was light and youthful. She turned and looked past me toward the mirror and smiled. She must have been smiling at her reflection, seen across the room. She was so beautiful, so shockingly, overwhelmingly beautiful, that my heart almost stopped. Her hair was jet black and bobbed; her skin was creamy white. Her lips were scarlet, her eyelashes long, her neck and jaw smooth and perfect and the scarlet of her fingernails matched the scarlet of her lips. Her eyes were big, dark and mischievous. She was wearing a blue dress with a short pleated skirt and shiny silk stockings with no shoes. She sat on the bed, still smiling.

I saw her with the eyes of a grown man who knows a beautiful woman when he sees one, and I saw her also with the eyes of a six-year-old child – an only child to whom his mother is the most wonderful thing in the world. The combined effect was devastating. I was hypnotized. I did not move a muscle.

Then she pulled up her dress lazily and began to unfasten her garters. When I saw the cream white of the insides of her thighs I felt for a moment as though I would faint. I had never seen anything so exciting in my life. I remained frozen in my little chair. She took her silk stockings off, laid them beside her on the bed's pink coverlet. The room was silent; from somewhere outside I could hear the chattering of a squirrel. For a moment I tried to turn my eyes away from the mirror, but I could not do it.

She stood up and, facing the window now so that she was reflected in profile, she began taking the dress off, pulling it over her head. She was wearing a short pink slip underneath.

Sometimes in my life I have wondered how it must feel to inject pure heroin into a vein. I think the pleasure would be electric in its intensity. I felt that now, looking at Mother through the eyes of both youth and age. There was, too, the sense of danger and of power that comes with seeing another intimately without being seen. There was the erotic joy of seeing a woman so beautiful, so self-absorbed, take off her clothes. And it was such a *forbidden* thing to see my mother expose her body. I could not take my eyes away – not while this heroin was in my blood.

She continued, as I knew by now she would. She pulled the slip slowly over her head, shook her lovely black hair back into order, and laid the slip on the bed by her hose. She was wearing pink silk step-ins and a lacy pink brassiere. Her figure was perfect and her skin perfectly white. I sat transfixed. The feelings in me were like a hurricane and my soul was in the eye of it. I felt frozen in the moment. I wanted to stay in it forever.

And then I heard her voice again as from a distance. It was softer now and a bit throaty. What she said was, 'Now be sure you don't peek, dear.' Then as I watched she bent and took off her panties. I saw the jet black of her pubic hair, so flawlessly seated in that charismatic V. I could see the tiny lips of her vagina, as pink as the coverlet on the bed, as pink as the wallpaper, as her slip, her panties. My heart pounded like a mallet in my chest and then as she removed her brassiere and stood there naked by the bed, still smiling, smiling now toward where I sat upright in my little chair, I felt a swooning inside myself. The heroin had me. My vision blurred and I was back in Limbo.

I sat stunned for several moments. And then I felt a brief flash of anger shake my body. I felt *had*, in some fundamental way, felt pinned down and tormented by the tableau I had just lived through.

But the anger left me soon. I was washed out, vaguely

guilty, empty. I slept. I dreamed of Mother in her black wool coat in autumn when I was in the first grade. She would walk me carefully to school, helping me with the intersections. I dreamed of the way she would hold my right hand tightly in her left and I could feel the firm, metallic pressure of her engagement ring and her wedding ring. She would talk to me aimlessly of this and that – the weather, the new dresses she was going to buy – and I would hang on every word. I loved her terribly.

That was a long time ago in Limbo-time since I first went back to Mother's pink bedroom. I have stopped counting days and years here but I know that a great deal of time has passed.

Sometimes I feel restless and I yearn to finish the editing of my past so that I can be reborn to continue in whatever plan whatever god there is has made, and I feel that I know what needs to be done. I need to go back to Mother's bedroom and merely close my eyes and keep them closed. *I must not look in that mirror.*

And God knows I have tried. I have gone back there a hundred times and more, have sat in that chair and heard that soft and throaty voice saying, 'Now be sure you don't peek, dear,' and have stared at that face, those hips, those breasts, that lovely flesh. I have swooned, over and over. Her movements exist now in frozen choreography in my brain; they seem to have erased everything afterward in my one life so that the ten minutes in the bedroom when I was six years old are what that life was *for.* My swoon is like the hub around which the rest of my life revolves; should I change it the rest of my life might scatter into empty and frightening disorder.

Yet it would seem simple to close my eyes or turn them downward, only once, to render those ten minutes of my past null and void, so that I may move on to whatever other destiny waits for me – to that pleasant Beth I have wanted to be, in my warm home with dolls and a pet cat and children's books. I can feel at times the yearning of Beth within me wanting to become real and alive in the

171

world. And so I go back to the pink bedroom from time to time, but I cannot change a thing.

It is always the same: Mother. the bed. the small chair, the long mirror on the closet door. And I never close my eyes.

I pray sometimes to God that Beth, who will never live, will forgive me, for I cannot erase those ten minutes from my life no matter how many times I try. I truly cannot.

THE END

BATTLE CIRCLE
by Piers Anthony

Including *Sos The Rope – Var The Stick – Neq The Sword.*

In this highly imaginative trilogy, master science fiction
writer Piers Anthony creates a world of savage power, of
primitive and brutal laws where all disputes are settled in
the battle circle, and where men must seize and realise their
vision of an empire by the might of their primitive
weapons.

'Anthony's story of men fighting for mastery of wandering
tribes, with sword, club and robe in the ceremonial Great
Circle, has its own internal conviction – its own grandeur,
even . . . a rigorous masculine power, rare in any kind of
novel nowadays'
The Observer

0 552 99085 X   £3.95

MOCKINGBIRD
by Walter Tevis

'Every so often a science fiction novel emerges which belongs in the mainstream of literature, and Walter Tevis's *Mockingbird* is emphatically one such'
The Observer

A world where humans wander, drugged and lulled by electronic bliss. A dying world of no children, no art, no reading. A strange love triangle: Spofforth, the most perfect machine ever created, whose only wish is to die; Paul and Mary Lou, whose passion for each other is the only future. Some still refuse to surrender . . .

'An exciting and original book'
Punch

'An extremely ingenious and intelligent novel, much more than science fiction'
Yorkshire Post

'Exciting, epic and eventually very moving'
Sunday Telegraph

0 552 12356 0   £2.50

THE COOL WAR
by Frederick Pohl

Award-winning author of *Jem* and *Man Plus*.

A few years into the future, ostensibly all nations are at peace – but the world is falling apart. The Reverend H. Hornswell Hake, a Unitarian minister, is drafted – courtesy of the Lo-Wate Bottling Co – into a war he's never heard of – the cool war. The undercover war-makers are men and women who are creating havoc in rival countries. Without ever leaving evidence that their nation is responsible, they push drugs, import porno flicks, blight crops, cause droughts . . .

Hake's first brief is to take a party of children to France, Norway and Denmark to present marmosets to schools and youth groups. An innocent enough project – but as a result, sickness spreads throughout Western Europe. And this was only the beginning . . .

0 552 12153 3   £1.75

A SELECTED LIST OF SCIENCE FICTION AND FANTASY TITLES AVAILABLE FROM CORGI BOOKS

ORDER FORM

All these books are available at your bookshop or newsagent, or can be ordered direct from the publisher. Just tick the titles you want and fill in the form below.

CORGI BOOKS. Cash Sales Department. P.O. Box 11. Falmouth. Cornwall.

Please send cheque or money order, no currency.

Please allow cost of book(s) plus the following for postage and packing.

U.K. Customers—Allow 45p for the first book. 20p for the second book and 14p for each additional book ordered. to a maximum charge of £1.63.

B.F.P.O. and Eire—Allow 45p for the first book. 20p for the second book plus 14p per copy for the next seven books. thereafter 8p per book.

Overseas Customers—Allow 75p for the first book and 21p per copy for each additional book.

NAME (Block Letters) . . . .

ADDRESS . . . .

. . . .